Praise for

STOP THAT GIRL

"Ann Ransom [is] a funny, ferocious and intensely likable narrator. McKenzie is an accomplished humorist and a developed stylist, and she wastes no time dazzling the reader with her clean direct language, her simple but searing use of metaphor and her unflinching eye. . . . The paragraphs are put together with razor sharp concision, and the book is rich in both narrative and linguistic surprise. . . . An original."

—*The New York Times Book Review*

"Within fifteen pages Ann has broken Granny's arm and begun her discovery that the world is a wide and various place filled with all sorts of odd people with weird ideas and motives, which pretty much describes the world of the rest of these stories, populated by angry mothers, voracious boyfriends, laid-back California entrepreneurs, an odd Australian environmentalist. . . . Hilarious . . . Call these excerpts from a life you never dreamed of before reading about it . . . anti–fairy tales, stories that seem so true you'll say to yourself, 'Oh, these awful and sometimes lovely things must have actually happened.' That's always the mark of a convincing writer."

—ALAN CHEUSE, NPR's "All Things Considered"

"It would be easy to give up on the quirky, girly coming-of-age novel, except that when it works, there are few forms more pleasurable to read. And *Stop That Girl* works, on just about every level. . . . A lovely, funny, lucidly written account. . . . McKenzie's sentences are beautifully, cleanly made, with no excess nonsense. . . . She's single-handedly reinvigorated the coming-of-age genre. Here is a writer to watch, and a book to breeze through with glee." —*San Francisco Chronicle*

"[*Stop That Girl*] is full of such unexpected incidents—the damage is quirky but no less acute. . . . Candid, perceptive . . . [McKenzie's] tales flail with reckless energy. . . . Appealingly idiosyncratic, sharpened throughout by a keen sense of humor."
—*The Village Voice*

"Elizabeth McKenzie takes two difficult forms—the novel-in-stories and the coming-of-age tale—and makes them work brilliantly together. *Stop That Girl* is one of the funniest and smartest fiction debuts I've read in a long, long time."
—ROBERT OLEN BUTLER, author of *Had a Good Time*

"McKenzie's take on childhood is so smart, funny and fiercely observant. . . . [She delivers] such delicious paragraphs . . . Gets the youthful intimation of mortality down to perfection."
—*Los Angeles Times Book Review*

"Deftly captures one woman's life . . . A fine first book, alive with energy, wit, and real promise." —*Kirkus Reviews*

"Vibrant and clear, these connected stories present a portrait of a family whose members are funny and hurtful and real, and watching them touched by time and change is very affecting. There is a lovely expansiveness here; surrounding the humor is the recognition that life is a serious deal."
—ELIZABETH STROUT, author of *Abide with Me*

"[McKenzie] *is* funny and her stories are wry and tuned to pop culture and politics. They inspire fantasies about being her best friend."   —*East Bay Express*

"A deliciously intelligent novel, funny and original and exact. McKenzie has a wonderful eye—and a relishing appetite—for the craziness that's everywhere in ordinary things if you know how to look."
    —TESSA HADLEY, author of *Everything Will Be All Right*

"Why is it such a kick to read Elizabeth McKenzie's *Stop That Girl*? Certainly Ann Ransom, the impulsive schoolgirl who comes of age in these interconnected tales, has more than her share of heartbreak. . . . Ann embraces life with a wary insight that couldn't be more engaging. A smart, swift-paced debut."
    —*O: The Oprah Magazine*

"Starting with a mynah bird who says 'Kill me!,' Ann Ransom views her world with mordant glee. Reading *Stop That Girl* was like remembering a life I've never lived—a lucid, wistful pleasure of the keenest sort."
    —RACHEL CLINE, author of *What to Keep*

"[A] delightful novel about a girl growing up in the mosh pit of family . . . Ann is wise beyond her years; she's also a wiseacre. Her rebellious, buoyant nature gilds her words as well as her deeds. . . . Smart girls everywhere will see themselves in Ann's smart mouth. Still—it's Ann in action that hallmarks this irrepressibly upbeat coming-of-age novel. . . . [*Stop That Girl*] leads us to consider our own childhoods, and it does in a way that is both poignant and optimistic."
    —*Santa Cruz Sentinel*

"Unsentimental; its young narrator looks at the world through an oddball's eyes; she dispenses with consoling illusions early. The writing has a cool economy, too."

—*Chicago Tribune*

"As is eminently apparent from the elegant style, sharp wit, and captivating voice in *Stop That Girl,* there will be no stopping Elizabeth McKenzie in her literary career. This is a superb book."   —JENNY MCPHEE, author of *No Ordinary Matter*

"Shockingly assured . . . What's most wonderful about these thoroughly entertaining stories is how subtle they are."

—*San Francisco* magazine

"How about a coming-of-age story with a little imagination? . . . Ann's voice and sensibility give the book an extra touch of fun. (Dig the car chase that involves an estranged grandmother and Allen Ginsberg.) Stop that girl? When you get a load of her, you definitely won't want to."

—*Daily Candy* (Los Angeles)

"*Stop That Girl* runs at breakneck speed from beginning to end; this is a wildly original, unforgettable debut, funny and poignant and perfect for anyone who has survived childhood."

—KATE WALBERT, author of *Our Kind*

"Ann Ransom is unstoppable. . . . McKenzie shows us that life is a series of stories that are linked like chains. . . . Ann tells us of her eventful life in a matter-of-fact, deadpan voice—often wildly funny but just as often thoughtful and sad—that will appeal to both adults and YAs."   —*Booklist*

STOP THAT GIRL

Random House

Trade Paperbacks

New York

STOP THAT GIRL

Fiction

Elizabeth McKenzie

2006 Random House Trade Paperback Edition

Copyright © 2005 by Elizabeth McKenzie
Reading group guide copyright © 2005
by Random House, Inc.

Published in the United States by
Random House Trade Paperbacks, an imprint of
The Random House Publishing Group, a division
of Random House, Inc., New York.

RANDOM HOUSE TRADE PAPERBACKS and colophon
are trademarks of Random House, Inc.

READER'S CIRCLE and colophon are trademarks
of Random House, Inc.

Originally published in hardcover in the
United States by Random House, an imprint of
The Random House Publishing Group, a division
of Random House, Inc., in 2005.

Some of the stories in this book first appeared in the
following publications: "Stop That Girl" in ZYZZYVA and
Best American Nonrequired Reading 2002; "The Possible
World" in Threepenny Review and Pushcart Prize XXV;
"We Know Where We Are, But Not Why" in Other Voices.

LIBRARY OF CONGRESS
CATALOGING-IN-PUBLICATION DATA

McKenzie, Elizabeth
Stop that girl: a novel in stories / Elizabeth McKenzie.
p.   cm.
ISBN 0-8129-7228-7
1. Girls—Fiction.   2. Young women—Fiction.
3. Grandmothers—Fiction.   4. Mothers and daughters—
Fiction.   5. Children of divorced parents—Fiction.
6. United States—Social life
and customs—Fiction.   I. Title.

PS3613.C556S76 2005
813'.6—dc22   2004050873]

Printed in the United States of America

www.thereaderscircle.com

2 4 6 8 9 7 5 3 1

Book design by Dana Leigh Blanchette

To my family,
and to the memory
of my mother

CONTENTS

STOP THAT GIRL

Stop That Girl

My mother and I lived alone then, in a pink bungalow in Long Beach, with a small yard full of gopher holes and the smell of the refinery settling over everything we had. We couldn't leave our glasses on the shelves a week without them gathering a fine mist of oil. I thought we had a real life anyway, before my mother started over.

We employed a stocky Yorkshire woman to walk me home from school past the barbershop with the unhappy mynah bird. "Kill me!" it suggested as we passed by.

I never knew my father. Named Ransom, he was some frat boy who danced well. Mom believed I'd have a leveler head.

My mother worked in petroleum research. She was a geology major in college and went to field camps in Wyoming and was renowned for shooting a bobcat at a hundred yards while it was cuffing around her professor's beagle. For the oil company, she looked through telescopes at the moon, as if there might be something useful up there. Mom felt her job was a joke. When she came home at night, she locked herself in the bathroom for an hour, taking a hot bath filled with salts.

She was said to look like Lauren Bacall in those days and dated a few of the engineers from the refinery. While Mom went searching for her purse and coat, they would bribe me with something, like it was up to me to release her: Silly Putty, a magnet, a comic book, a stuffed pig with a music box in it.

There we are in Long Beach the fall I'm nearly eight, when the nights have grown cooler and our gas wall unit bangs out its stale-smelling heat, and we're on the brink of changes so vast it's hard to believe we don't see them coming. One Saturday evening, we receive a new visitor in the form of Roy Weeks, a real estate broker, a handsome talker with dimples, cowboy boots, and a rounded ruby ring that looks like a bloody eyeball. He brings a bouquet as big as a baby, and my mother holds it that way. He slips me a piece of Dubble Bubble. By the following week it's a Slip 'N Slide. I suspect he appeals to that secret Wild West part of my mother, but it's more. A few months later my mother tells me, "Roy's taking us both out for a drive today, Ann. We're going to see a house."

I sit in the backseat of Roy's Pontiac as we leave Long Beach behind. We aim for the San Fernando Valley. "You mean we're going to buy a house out here?" I ask Mom.

We're in the Encino hills; compared to Long Beach it looks like paradise. Huge ranch houses and big yards; rosebushes, hibiscus, banana trees, palms.

"Well, maybe," my mother says, turning around in her seat like she has something to tell me. "We might buy a house—with Roy."

"*From* Roy?"

"No, with him. We might all live out here together."

"Ann, are you ready for that?" Roy says, eyeing me in his mirror.

I realize what they're trying to tell me.

We pull up in front of a huge, shingled yellow house, as long as the entire row of bungalows in Long Beach. My mother looks stunned as we wander into the place. It has beamed ceilings, parquet floors, a kitchen with an island and double range, a breakfast nook and bar, a family room, three bedrooms, three baths, two fireplaces, and a den. They show me the room that would be mine; it has sheer pink curtains and wallpaper with ballerinas on it, something for a well-defined girl. When we finish inspecting the place, Roy Weeks says, "Ann, hit me right here! As hard as you can!" He is pointing at his stomach.

I don't ask why. I just do it.

"I'm waiting." He winks at my mother.

My hand hurts. I kick him in the shin.

Nine months later, Mrs. Weeks has retired from petroleum work, pregnant. In the afternoons, in our new palace, she sews clothes and toys and bedding for the baby, placing them in the nursery-to-be, while I'm thinking of names. Percy is the one I'm rooting for.

Quiet collects in the rooms of that big house more than anywhere we've lived. I often tell my mother it's a tomb, and she says, "Ann, I love this man. But you are still the most important person in the world to me"—the words I live for—and I skate around the parquet floor in my socks, still feeling like it's all just temporary. I still can't believe that another family has moved into the pink bungalow, that the woman I called Nana has returned to Leeds, and that a few friends from my school in Long Beach write me real letters with stamps on them like I've moved across the world.

"How about a swim?" Mom asks me after school nowadays.

"Maybe."

I come out into the backyard after a while and see my mother, in her white flowered bathing cap, doing graceful laps up and down the pool. This is no kidney-shaped job, as Roy points out. It's a classic rectangle of crystal blue, and my eyes follow the long wake of my mother's stroke.

"Come on in," Mom calls to me.

To surprise my mother, I say "Okay" and walk straight into the pool with all my clothes on. She laughs and doesn't get mad at me for possibly ruining my leather shoes. It's in the afternoons after school when I know I still have an impact on her. Once Roy's home, she acts like he's our savior.

One evening he insists we accompany him to some

open-house thing, and I climb onto the roof of the Pontiac and won't get off.

"Get down, Ann," my pregnant mother says, waiting swaybacked by the car. Roy snaps at my ankles like a crab.

"From up here I can see the reservoir," I say. "I think boys are peeing into it."

"That's nice; let's go."

"Is that, like, what we drink?"

Roy stalks around the car and I hop to the other side. He charges back, and this time I slip off. I fall onto the concrete and no matter how much it hurts I decide I won't cry. Instead I pretend I'm in a coma.

"Ann?" my mother says. "Are you all right? Look what you did!" she yells at Roy Weeks.

"Faker," he replies. He tickles me.

I sink my teeth into his arm. He slaps me across the top of the head, and my mother tells Roy never to lay a hand on me again. Roy tells my mother I'm becoming a spoiled brat, and then I sit up and hear myself saying, "And *you're* a homewrecker."

And thus, the following weekend, it's decided I'm spending some time with The Frosts. The Frosts are my grandparents, but when we talk about them we always call them The Frosts. Until then, I'd only seen them once or twice a year because my mother hates them. They are young and have busy schedules for grandparents—Sherwood's a civil engineer, Liz a pediatrician. Mom grew up a lonely daydreamer with no brothers or sisters. That's her rationale for the new baby: so things will be different for me.

Friday afternoon Dr. Frost shows up to collect me. She

looks like my mother but is smaller and more efficient, never a moment to kill. I don't know her very well. "Put on a dress with a nice collar, Ann. And comb your hair. I want you to look pretty for your passport."

"Why do I need a passport?"

"Hasn't your mother told you about our trip?"

"What trip?"

"You're coming to Europe with me. I'm attending a medical conference. You're going to straighten out and learn your place in the world. Good deal?"

"Europe?" I say, looking at my mother. "When?"

"Next month," Dr. Frost says.

Next month is May. May is a big month. May is when Mom is having the baby.

"I can't go," I say. "I need to be here for the baby."

"You've been a big help already," my mother says.

"I need to help more!"

Dr. Frost says, "After we have your picture taken, let's go buy some new clothes, shall we? I'm going to need some new things myself."

"I don't need any new clothes."

"All right, then, we'll just get your picture taken," Dr. Frost says.

I'm speechless, but finally I say, "This is definitely bizarre and grotesque," my favorite expression in many situations. Then I add my other: "It's also grossly mutilated and hugely deformed."

"Ann, your grandmother has offered to take you to Europe. You're a very lucky girl."

Lucky? Who needs parquet floors and a pool. Who needs Europe with the very person who makes my mother scream or cry whenever they talk on the phone. I try to catch my mother's eye, the special eye that knows me better than anyone, and say, "I don't want to go." But the eye doesn't blink. There's no hope. Though they disagree on everything else, they're together on this one. Mom tells me, "The baby might not even come while you're gone, who knows."

Roy can't make it to the airport. Neither can Granddad. I hug my mother and pat her stomach, which looks square now, like a little house. "Tell Percy to wait," I croak out.

"I'll try," my mother says.

Our travels take us first to Copenhagen, city of copper domes turned green and raw beef. I'm in Europe. I'm excited. I tell myself I'll see yodelers and eat lots of chocolate and buy souvenirs for my mother and the people I've been meeting at my new school. Even Dr. Frost seems to have loosened up. She's humming and smiling without explaining why.

Our second night there, in a quaint hotel with floors tilted like a fun house, we receive a telegram from Roy Weeks:

WONDERFUL NEWS STOP WE HAVE A DAUGHTER KATHERINE LOUISE STOP MOTHER AND BABY FINE.

"Who's *we*?" I say, grabbing the telegram. It hits me for the first time that my sister's father is *Roy Weeks*. "Can I call Mom at the hospital?"

Dr. Frost says we'll send a telegram instead.

"Can we go home now?"

"Ann, you don't want to see a newborn baby. They're ugly little things with red faces. They don't even open their eyes."

"Really?"

I slide in my socks to the lower wall. Tivoli Gardens sparkles across the street. From her bag my grandmother hauls out a textbook she has brought on this trip to instruct me with. It contains pictures of every bone, every muscle, every lymph gland; the cardiovascular, digestive, and nervous systems: the works. "Tell me about dissecting cadavers," I ask her.

"Nothing to it," Dr. Frost says.

"But you were cutting open dead bodies. Wasn't it bizarre and grotesque?"

"Ann, the body is an amazing machine. It's not bizarre and grotesque at all." She points at a skeleton.

I want to hear exciting stories about guts, not her cooled down version of them. "Dead bodies are wonderful, newborn babies are really gross?"

"Good night, Ann," she says.

"Maybe we should go home," I murmur, but she ignores me in a different way, pretending not to hear. I pull the covers up around my neck and fall asleep, hearing my grandmother listing bones.

The International College of Surgeons is meeting in Vienna, and we take three days driving there through Germany. I like stopping in towns and villages, bounding around cobblestone squares, dipping my hands in fountains, and eating pastries. I decide to stop thinking about home. The afternoon we arrive in Vienna we check in at the Intercontinental across from the park, in plenty of time for the first night's event, and I'm fitting right in. Dr. Frost takes a long bath and changes into a blue chiffon dress, and I wear a green velvet frock with white gloves, and we set out for our evening together in a taxicab. She smells like hairspray and Chanel No. 5 and talcum all mixed together. Her rings glint in the summer evening light. She taps her little heels.

We pull up at a real palace and proceed up a bank of marble steps. The roar of the doctors from around the globe deepens as we get closer. Dr. Frost grabs the list of those in attendance and scans it. When we cross into the ballroom I look up at my grandmother and she has her nose at full tilt, her forehead high like a half moon. A small orchestra is tuning up at the end of the room. Dr. Frost taps me on the shoulder and points to a tall silvery-haired man standing alone in the crowd. "Go introduce yourself to that man," she urges me.

"Why?"

"Just do it," she whispers.

Luckily I don't have to, because he turns and his face is

radiant at the sight of Dr. Frost. "Liz," he says. He gives her a kiss and looks at her and laughs. "And this is your daughter?"

"My *granddaughter*," she says.

"Impossible," he says, taking her hand. "You look wonderful."

"Ann, this is Dr. Von Allsberg," she tells me.

I'm more interested in what's for dinner, and I locate our table next to the dance floor. Eventually a doctor takes the seat next to me, while Dr. Frost talks to the man with the silver hair. My doctor has a waxed mustache and smells like varnish. His name is Dr. Witkovitch and he's an internist from a small village in the Julian Alps. He tells me he breeds roller pigeons, which come in all colors and are iridescent. They rocket high into the sky, then come rolling down to earth in a free fall. It's a stunt and they enjoy it. I realize that Dr. Witkovitch is actually a very young man; it's the stiff mustache, oiled hair, and musty jacket that make him seem outdated and old. I'm thinking Dr. Frost will be impressed to see that I've befriended someone so quickly, but she's not watching. We turn to our plates and slice up thin wafers of veal.

Later the orchestra plays Strauss and I watch while Dr. Von Allsberg waltzes with Dr. Frost. She moves like a swan, head back and eyes fastened on him.

"How do you know Dr. Von Allsberg?" I ask her that night.

"I know many people here."

"Can we go to Dr. Witkovitch's roller-pigeon farm?"

"Hardly," she says, examining her eyes in the mirror. "We have plenty to do as it is."

"Not even for a day?"

"Where is it?"

"Yugoslavia," I tell her.

"Ha!"

The next day Dr. Frost leaves me with a babysitting service at the hotel. Over the phone, arranging it, someone calls her Mrs. Frost. "It's *Dr.* Frost," she replies. She never lets that mistake slip by. "Whenever your grandfather makes reservations for Dr. and Mr. Frost, they behave very peculiarly, because they assume your grandfather must be the doctor and therefore is married to a man. People would rather believe your grandfather is *married to a man* than think *a woman is a doctor!*"

I am shocked.

"Say, after the conference we'll take a boat trip on the Danube together; how would that be?" she asks me.

"Good," I say.

"Better than a bunch of roller chickens?"

"Pigeons!"

"Same difference."

The babysitter is a glum old Austrian woman who feeds me hard salty meat in a broth with gray dumplings bobbing around in it, and snaps *It-is-not-allowed!* every time I move. By pointing at the park and annoying her with long sentences she doesn't understand, I get her to take me on a walk, but I'm in such a bad mood I end up throwing rocks at a swan. And I'm disappointed Dr. Witkovitch hasn't hunted me down to find out if I can visit his farm in Yugoslavia.

The last night in Vienna, the night we are supposed to go to a special Hungarian restaurant and sample goulash, my grandmother breaks the news to me she's going to an opera with Dr. Von Allsberg instead.

"You can come too, of course," she tells me. "But I promise you, it will be very long and boring."

"In that case, I'd love to."

"Seriously, Ann, I don't think you'd enjoy it. I'm all for exposing you to cultural events, but you'll have a lot more fun running around here."

"Running around?" This makes me grind my teeth, and I close my eyes and imagine my grandmother being speared by headhunters. "What's the opera, anyway?"

"*Der Rosenkavalier,*" she tells me. Then she proceeds to offer up the whole story, which is about mistaken identities. If she already knows, why does she need to go? And I'm skeptical about the plot. People can't be tricked that easily. If I went home in a costume, my mother would still recognize me. It's changes on the inside she won't be able to see.

There's a different babysitter at night, an old bald man with only a pinky and thumb on his right hand. I keep rushing to the window and looking out at the lamps in the park and then at every cab pulling up, to see if my grandmother is returning. At last, very late, I see Dr. Frost and Dr. Von Allsberg strolling together out of the park, their heads close and crowned by lamplight. And it's bizarre and grotesque because I can see that they're holding hands.

When the conference ends, I'm glad to see the last of Von Allsberg. My grandmother and I drive to a small village on the Danube where we board the promised boat. It's a hot May day. We spend hours drifting past castles and abbeys and orchards, sitting on the deck in the sun eating little Napoleons and drinking tea. This is what I've been waiting for.

"I wish there had been more women there for you to meet," my grandmother remarks. "You're to do great things. No man should stand in your way. And don't let Roy Weeks tell you otherwise! Think you'd like to be a doctor?" she asks.

"Maybe. What about industrial baking?"

"I want you to set your sights as high as you can. Your mother was sent to fine schools. I don't want you to think—" She pauses. "Don't ever let them change your name. I happen to know the Ransoms are a very fine family."

I narrow my eyes to the sun. "And what's a fine family like?"

"A fine family, Ann, is one with noble values and good ancestry. Like mine. Congressmen, attorneys and judges, officers in the Civil and Revolutionary wars. Well educated and able to contribute to society."

"And did they get along with their kids?"

"They passed along the right things," she said. "I'm glad you and I are getting to know each other. Your mother was what they call a daddy's girl. Never liked me, even as a baby."

I look to see if Dr. Frost is kidding. "Babies love their mothers."

"Not in this case. I'm afraid you've no idea what I'm talking about, coming from the pickle she put you in."

And I say, "Well, I'm afraid you have no idea what I'm talking about, because Mom says all you ever cared about was yourself."

"I see." Dr. Frost snorts.

For the rest of the boat ride, when I'm not snapping pictures in every direction, I'm trying to make my grandmother forget what I've said. My new sister might entice her. "She's much nicer than I am," I say. "She has red hair and speaks many languages. She can do magic tricks and dance."

"There'll be no stopping you two," my grandmother replies.

And finally, the day reaches its obvious conclusion when we get off the boat and Dr. Von Allsberg stands waiting on the dock with flowers. "Why didn't you tell me he was going to be here?"

"Seriously, Ann. Are you my keeper?"

I march behind them, filtering everything I see at the little port on the river through a blaze of fury. Spears are flying, and Dr. Frost is being lowered into a boiling cauldron. Tears are filling my eyes and I don't want anyone to see them. Suddenly, I get a singular urge to run up behind her and jump on her back, screaming *"Piggyback ride!"* Wham. Her small efficient body tumbles and cracks on the cobblestones.

"God!" she groans.

"Sorry," I say, standing up.

"What were you thinking?" Von Allsberg says.

"Ulna's fractured," Dr. Frost announces.

"Faker!" I say.

"Afraid not," she says.

We spend hours in a local clinic while they set her arm. It's a clean break. A neurologist, Von Allsberg supervises the exam, pricking her fingertips and banging a tuning fork on his shoe and then pressing the cool metal to her elbow and palms. How could a bone break so easily? Lying on the table, in the sallow light of the clinic, she looks old, finally—the way a grandmother should.

Now everything is different. My grandmother can't drive the car—not with a gearshift and a broken right arm—so Dr. Von Allsberg offers to get us back to Copenhagen. We'll spend just a few more days in Germany and Holland. I'm now stuck in the backseat, where I have to stare at their necks. They talk and laugh and occasionally toss comments back to me like bits for a stray dog. Dr. Frost has bumps and creases on her neck; does Dr. Von Allsberg realize? Somewhere along the way, Von Allsberg buys me a doll—an Alpine girl in a dirndl, clutching a little straw basket—and I immediately detest her like I detest the ballerinas in my room at home. But I have to admit, she's in a beautiful box. The box is green and has a delicate pattern on it and is lined with velvet.

It's the polar route home, twelve hours flying over fields of ice, and it's important to make sure Dr. Frost is as comfortable as possible. There's no doubt, her arm hurts. She takes the window seat so she won't be jostled, and the cast rolls between us with no one's signature on it except mine. I can't wait to get home.

At last we land in Los Angeles. I'm so excited I forget my carry-on bag and have to run back into the plane. Finally, walking out of customs, beaming with my experiences, returning to my homeland, I spot my mother and Roy in the crowd. They are waving, watching our glorious arrival. They are standing with a baby buggy.

"Mom!" I yell, running to her.

"Hello, Ann!" Roy Weeks says, hugging me first.

I get to my mother. I had imagined her grabbing me and squeezing me like there was no tomorrow, but she looks deflated somehow, an imposter in my mother's clothing. "Mom?"

"Mother, your arm!" she says.

"Hello, Helen," Dr. Frost says. "Is this my new granddaughter?"

"Mom, I have a present for you!" I say, digging into my bag.

Everyone's peering into the buggy. I decide to wait on the souvenirs and wiggle in for a look. I see my sister for the first time. She's very small, surrounded by the blankets my mother made. She's wearing the yellow cap I sewed the piping on. I reach in to pick her up.

"No, dear," my mother says. "Not now. She's sleepy. Just leave her there."

I want to hold her.

"Ann, pay attention to your mother," Roy says. "You don't know how to hold her yet."

By then I am holding her just fine. "Percy," I say.

"Let me have her," my mother says.

"Just a second."

"Hand over the little one," orders Dr. Frost.

"Ann, give her to me *now*," says Mom.

That's it. I start to run. After carrying my suitcase all over Europe, she's only a tiny bundle.

My mother says, "Wait! Stop!"

It was the beginning of my future, and I had the thought at that moment there was no one in the world who would ever understand my version of things. I plunged through the crowd, holding my sister close to me. I heard my mother crying out, my grandmother barking commands, and Roy Weeks shouting, "Stop that girl!" But no one seemed to connect them to me, so no one stood in my way.

After tearing down a flight of stairs and rounding a few corners, I found a vacant phone booth and closed the two of us in. My sister wasn't frightened. Why should she be? I held her out carefully and looked at her puffy blue eyes. She was staring right at me. Like she really wanted to know who I was and what would become of us. Though she had almost no hair or eyebrows, she looked exactly the way I'd imagined her. She lifted a small fist to her mouth and started sucking on it. "It's me," I taught her. "It's Ann. Ann. Ann."

It was a good thing I was home. My sister was growing up.

Hope Ranch

The world was opening up for me. I was friends with every kid on the block. I made my rounds. I burned garbage in an incinerator with Cindy and Greg, played tetherball with Joan, sang folk songs on an autoharp with Melanie, hid out in a "bomb shelter" with Janet. I threw rocks at Kevin, David, and Tom and climbed trees with Malcolm. I knew every square in the sidewalk. Some had X's in them. Those were Monkey Squares. Leslie and I walked home from school together and we hopped over those.

My sister was two all of a sudden, a pudgy, cheerful two, a messy dishwater blonde with a cowlick, and I was rushing home with a new Creeple-People head for her, a really ugly one made especially for her by a kid in my class with his own Creeple-People factory, when my grandmother, Dr. Frost, pulled up alongside me in her black Corvette convertible. The top was off. "Hop on in," she called. It was a two-seater. There wasn't room for Leslie.

"I didn't know you were coming," I said.

"Well, here I am. Get in."

"See you tomorrow." I waved to Leslie.

"Bye." Leslie waved.

"Don't think you will," Dr. Frost said, as we zipped away.

"Why not?"

To my surprise, she passed my street and continued on, in the direction of the freeway.

"Wait, aren't we going home?"

"I've already packed your things; you're all ready to go," she said. "Now pipe down. We have a lot to talk about."

"But I'm giving this to Kathy!"

Dr. Frost wrinkled her nose without even looking at the rubbery head. "She has more toys than any human child needs."

"And I'm supposed to be working on my Theodore Roosevelt report, which is due Monday, and I'm invited to Jody Gunn's house today. *For the first time.*"

"My heart bleeds," she said.

"It *should* bleed!"

"Poor ol' Mumsy," she said, in that fake accent I detested. "Why's everyone always pickin' on me?"

"And why do I have to call you Mumsy?" I said.

"Because I called my grandmother Mumsy, and so did my mother, and so on. What's wrong with it?"

"Why can't I call you Granny, or Grandma, or Gran?"

"I never want to be called those things. They're what you call an old washerwoman."

I hated having to call anyone *Mumsy.* So I thought of her as Dr. Frost or just *the Doctor.* Last time, Mom told me, "The Doctor is coming to get you tomorrow. It's not particularly convenient, but I don't know how to say no. She emotionally pulverizes me."

And I'd said, "What if *I* emotionally pulverize you?"

And she'd said, "You'll have learned from the best."

Now Dr. Frost was driving too fast for my comfort. I asked her to slow down.

"What's wrong, can't stand a little excitement?"

"I feel carsick," I said.

"Hold on to your hat and watch the road."

My grandmother was passing everyone else on the highway, even driving on the shoulder when necessary. My hair was whipping around my head, and my lips were chapping faster than I could lick them.

"We're gonna beat the light!" Dr. Frost shouted into the din. "I'm not stopping until we get there."

"I'm hungry," I said.

"Dig around in the back. I brought a little picnic."

I was afraid to unloosen the seat belt and look, as if I'd fly out of the car. I groped behind me and found a paper bag and pulled it up to the front. In it was a shriveled head of celery, a blackened pear, three pieces of Roman Meal bread with mold on the edges, and a rind of cheese that was as hard as a hood ornament. I felt around to see if there was anything else. There wasn't.

"Can't we stop to eat?" I said.

"Ann, life is tough," she shouted. "Get used to it!"

●

We followed the coast road north and ended up in Santa Barbara just under two hours later. Still no time for a square meal. We pulled off the highway and zoomed under an arch welcoming us to HOPE RANCH, past an artificial lake full of birds, a golf course, and a number of large houses with iron gates or circular drives, and then disappeared into an oak forest in a ravine climbing a hill. "I've picked every house your grandfather and I ever lived in," she said. "I have an eye. You start with the best area. Then you find a place a little off-market, a little tattered around the edges. In other words, not a showcase. If you buy a place like that in the best part of town, you'll never go wrong."

I filed away her real estate tip for later. "So, you and Granddad are moving up here?"

"Your grandfather and I are finished."

"Finished? Good." One of my grandfather's hobbies was refinishing wood. He often talked about the finish on various objects. I thought she was saying that she and Grandad were all shiny and fixed up.

We drove on, pulling out of the grove of oaks into a countrylike area with no sidewalks, just horse paths by the road. We turned onto a short dead-end street and pulled up beside a dark hedge and a heavy iron gate. "Open it, Ann. It's unlocked."

I did as told. Still couldn't see any house. The air smelled of pine sap and rotting leaves. I trotted back to the car and climbed in, and the Doctor and I roared up the driveway and parked outside a garage with a rumpled door, paint peeling in curly little strips.

"You and Granddad will have to refinish it," I said.

Dr. Frost glared at me. "Weren't you listening? I just told you, we're finished."

"What do you mean?"

"I'm never spending another night under the same roof as that man, as long as I live, is what I mean," Dr. Frost said.

"You're sick of Granddad?"

"I certainly am. Now let's grab our bags and get inside."

I could hardly take this in. My grandfather was my favorite. He liked to fly his own plane and hunt for uranium in the desert with a Geiger counter. He laughed when I told him things. I'd describe kids at school and he'd draw cartoons of them, and I'd end up laughing so hard I would wheeze and snort like a donkey.

I followed her up a mossy brick walkway, and through the foliage, in the dimming light, I could at last see the house. It was a long Spanish-style place, with flowerpot tiles on the roof and thick plaster walls. The heavy wooden door was fringed with old brass hinges and had a tarnished knocker the shape of a lion's head. She fumbled with her keys and the slab creaked open, the dark house emitting a cool, musty draft like from a cave.

"Electricity's not on yet," she said. "Here." She poked a flashlight at me, an old crusty one with a failing beam unless I held it at precisely the right angle. Thus equipped, we started our tour, moving through the house room by room. There was a large formal dining room with oak plank floors, lamps shaped like candles on the wall, and a large picture window. Through a swinging door was the "butler's pantry." In my ray it looked like a kitchen, with its sink and dishwasher and counters and cupboards, but through another swinging door was the real kitchen. Then to a laundry room, with multiple sinks and bins and two built-in ironing boards, and a back bedroom and bath, which the Doctor called "the maid's quarters." It had a bell on the wall, and she said we could ring it from any room in the house.

"Are you going to have a maid?"

"Are you joking? I spent every penny I have on this place. Do you have any idea what that man has done to me?"

"No."

"I think you're old enough to hear these things. It's realistic. Life as it really happens. No girl should grow up in a fairy tale. You know where he was, when I was nearly dead in the Chicago Lying-In Hospital that winter, after having a cesarean with no anesthesia? Your mother being ten pounds nearly killed me. You know where he was?"

"How would I?"

"He was out in Denver, Colorado, living with some homosexual. Oh, he never admitted it, but there he was, taking a new job just before the baby was due, and next thing I find out he's shacking up with a man. And I know what kind of man this man was."

"What man?"

"Then he lied to me and said he was living alone. And

then he completely lost interest in you-know-what. Couldn't admit what he was, that's part of the problem. Was ashamed of himself."

"I'm hungry," I said.

"And I lived with it, thirty more years. Like nothing was wrong. Mending his socks, doing his laundry, even while I was in medical school, with all that work of my own."

"I'm *really* hungry."

"Come on then," she said, and I followed her back through the dark house, past the front entryway, past a living room that looked, in my sweeping beam, the size of a gymnasium. Then down a long pitch-black hall past several empty bedrooms and bathrooms until we came to the last and largest bedroom, which now had two cots in it and a number of boxes and suitcases. "This will be our headquarters until the furniture comes," she told me.

"When?"

"Next Tuesday."

"I'm not staying until then!"

"We have many things to do. Time will fly."

"But we're having a quiz Friday about protons and electrons!"

"You won't miss anything. I can teach you more in an hour than you'll learn all week. Now help me open this box."

I held the light while she pried open a large shipping box. In it were hundreds of cellophane-wrapped free samples of zwieback baby biscuits, and she ran her fingers through them with pleasure, like a crazed pirate fondling her doubloons.

"Baby biscuits?" I said.

"They're an excellent food."

I tore one open. It dissolved in my mouth like sand. "How old are these?"

"Don't be fussy," she replied.

I stood in the corner coughing out zwieback particles, while Dr. Frost bungled around her cot.

"In the morning the Hoopengarners are coming over. They have a daughter your age, and Dr. Hoopengarner is going to be a colleague. Helped me find my new office, on State Street."

I was pointing my flashlight at her head.

"This is a very important new beginning for me. They ain't through with me yet! When Dad died a few years ago, he didn't have much, but the little bit he left me went into this house. It's the first thing of my own I've had since I was a girl."

"Bully for you."

"What?"

"Bully. It's what Theodore Roosevelt used to say."

"Would you get that thing off me?" Dr. Frost said. "I brought some candles. Why don't you pull them out of that bag."

"Is there a phone here?"

"Nope. We're roughing it until we settle in." She lit the candles and placed them on the windowsill, and since I was feeling cold I climbed into the sleeping bag she'd unrolled on my cot. It smelled old and mildewy, and there was a towel folded up for my head.

"I want to go home as soon as possible," I said. "Probably tomorrow."

"Ann, we'll work out the best deal we can. You'll never fit in with your mother's new family; it's treachery. The school here is excellent. I've already met with the sixth-grade teacher. Katerina Hoopengarner will be in your class."

An uncomfortable feeling rippled through me. "I fit in fine. Why are you saying that?"

"With Weeks? That two-bit weasel?"

"Roy's not a two-bit weasel. He helps me with homework and he makes good pancakes. And he's sick of exploiting the land! He's getting a new job."

"Is that so? Where?"

"In a library," I told her.

In a doctorly way, which she must have practiced while visiting leper colonies in China the year before, she came over and sat on the edge of my cot. "Ann, you know I was the first person you saw when you were born. I was standing right there. You bonded to me. The way baby ducks bond, on sight. Even to a puppet the shape of a duck. Doesn't matter. You saw *me*. I had your mother when I was only twenty, so I'm young enough to be your mother. I'm not saying I was perfect, first time around. I was too young. And I had no idea what your grandfather would do to me. My God, bring a girl from a big warm family like mine into that cold industrial Ohio winter surrounded by a bunch of grim Germans with their strange traditions and horrible food? It was like a bad dream. Didn't see anything wrong with plopping me down there and taking off for his career.

The ego on that man could sink a ship. And your mother and I didn't get along that well, as I'm sure you know. It was tough. I'd take the train home anytime I could; Dad would make sure I had the fare.

"I'm going to let you in on a terrible secret. Your grandfather is an alcoholic. One whiff of gin and I tense up, remembering all the nights he put away half a pint. And then he'd become abusive and say all kinds of terrible things to me. Didn't want me to go to medical school, thought it would interfere with the running of his household. Sometimes he'd get home after a hard week and have his martini and then force himself on me. This was supposed to be married life. I can't say I recommend it, Ann." She patted me twice on the arm and returned to rustling her boxes and bags.

"Are you Mumsy?" I said. It suddenly occurred to me that she was an imposter.

"Of course I'm Mumsy."

"Are you sure you're Mumsy?"

"Pipe down now," she hissed.

"What *is* a mumsy?" The more I said it, the more horrible it sounded.

"Ann, go to sleep."

"I don't want you and Granddad to be finished."

"Even after what I've told you?"

"And why don't you like Kathy? You never bring her along or play with her or even say her name."

"Oh, I like her fine," Dr. Frost said. "But she doesn't need me like you do. I've been investing for you secretly,

my dear. I've put away some Standard Oil and some Johnson and Johnson and some AT and T. Not much, but it'll
grow. Should help you out later. Now good night!"

On the bare plaster wall, starting at the bottom right,
like hieroglyphics, a face, probably mine, with short messy
hair and two freaked-out eyes, and then a little head, my
sister's, and then Mom and Roy, and then Granddad; and
then favorite animals including giraffes and armadillos; then
all the internal organs I could think of, including the ap-
pendix and spleen; and then some of the words I'd learned
in my Teach Yourself Russian course: armchair, clothes
rack, very good! thank you!; and then rough outlines of the
states I'd gone to, including Utah and Washington and
New Mexico; and then cactuses I liked, including saguaro,
beavertail, and organ-pipe; and fruits I liked, including pome-
granates, guavas, and figs; and spices we had in the cupboard at home, like cumin, coriander, and cayenne; and a
picture of the boots I wanted, and a few of the outfits I
wanted; and a few tongue twisters. Then a ghost story:

> Once there were three nurses, and two didn't like the
> other because she was mean, and one day someone's
> arm got amputated and the mean nurse had to get rid of
> it, and later the other nurses opened the supply closet,
> and there was the mean nurse, holding the arm! *And
> she was grinning!!!!!*

And then a herd of cows with huge udders, massive udders bulging under tiny little cows, all in number-two pencil, rendered by flashlight during that long night, on my grandmother's bedroom wall.

●

She woke me in the morning. "Ann, wake up. Ann! My goodness gracious! How in the world—? You sly dog! What a creation! They'll be studying it for years! I shall treasure it always. My, my!"

I smiled with surprise. How she'd react to my masterpiece, I'd been uncertain.

"Up and at 'em and grab your notebook. I want to show you the garden," she said, charging back down the hall.

I dressed and followed her into an early morning yard filled with shadows and dew. Out the front door was an orchard of citrus trees rising in rows up the slow hill, and she showed me at least a dozen orange trees full of fruit, several lemons, a few grapefruit trees, and even a lime. I grabbed an orange, peeled it in two seconds flat, and gobbled it up. Then there was an avocado tree as wide as an airplane, its branches draped to the ground. "We'll have guacamole coming out our ears!" she said. "Look at this too, there are one, two, three peach trees, three plums, and a loquat. We'll make jam. I'll show you how to put it up."

I followed her down the brick walkway that skirted the house, and at the other end we stood before an enormous planted garden.

"Would you look at these matilija poppies?" she cried.

"Six feet high and rising. They call them fried-egg flowers. Can you see why?"

I nodded, looking at the huge white flowers with the big yellow centers.

"How do you spell that?" I asked.

"M-a-t-i-l-i-j-a," she repeated for me, and I wrote it down in my book.

I still have that list. In surprisingly childish cursive, considering how mature I thought I was at the time, it names jade plants, lantana, hens-and-chickens, holly, Norfolk Island pine, date palms, cypress, birds-of-paradise, and many more. I remember clearly following her around the property, which she told me was three acres, to every corner of it. "Look at the nasturtiums, will you?" she said gleefully, over in one far corner. There was nearly a meadow of the round-leafed orange and yellow flowers. "You can eat these," she told me, and tore a leaf off and put it right into her mouth. "Try it!" she goaded me. "Go on!"

It was peppery, like a radish. I ate a few more.

"Try a flower," she said. I was hungry and tried some of those too. "We can spread these everywhere; look how big the seeds are." She showed me the nut-sized seeds, and I began to collect them in my pockets.

Paths wound through the grounds, and there were new specimens to be found at every turn. "Camellia, rhododendron, and azalea, all in the shade," she said. "Doing beautifully. Everything grows here. It's a superb Mediterranean climate, despite the occasional coastal fog. Oh, my lord, to top it off, there's a macadamia nut tree. Can you imagine? I didn't see it before."

I wrote it down.

"This is Eden! This is heaven on earth! Now inside, to change your clothes. The Hoopengarners are coming soon. Something nice."

"Then can I go home?" I asked.

"Let's give a call tonight, all right?"

It was a place to start.

●

The morning sun spilled in the window like paint. To warm my feet, I stood in a patch of it, until the sound of two angry voices reached me in a snarling rush. A peep through the bedroom window showed me my mother on the front porch; Mom had come to get me! But my mother was shouting at Dr. Frost and Dr. Frost was shouting just as much.

Slam went the front door, *bang* clattered a fist. Yells and cries made it sound like they were wrestling each other. Something smashed. Glass tinkled on the floor. Footsteps thundered down the hallway, and then Mom stood panting in the doorway, beholding me cowering on the cot at the base of my beautiful wall. "Oh, my God, did you do that?"

"I think it's spectacular," Dr. Frost said, right behind. "Do you know anything about children? *Do you?*"

"Get up," Mom said, grabbing up my clothes. "We're leaving."

"Aren't you happy to see me?" I said.

"I'll be happy to see you later," she said.

"Ann, tell your mother," Dr. Frost said. "Tell her about our plan. You have a say in this."

"That's ridiculous," Mom said. "Of course she doesn't have a say, she's a child. Put your shoes on!"

"Ann is like my daughter. More than you are. Why should she have to grow up with that gooney-bird you brought home? Give her a decent chance, for God's sake."

"Stop fighting!" I yelled.

Mom had my bag and was leading me by the arm, past Dr. Frost.

"Ann?" Dr. Frost said. "Ann. Speak up!"

With my mother's arm around me, I couldn't look back.

"Mom, let go. *Stop!*"

We stepped out the front door, into the sun.

"She's telling you to stop!" Dr. Frost shouted. She attempted to grab my mother. My mother shrugged her off and kept moving ahead, holding on to my shoulders.

"Mom, talk to her!"

She bent, face-to-face with me, mouth tight as a bottle top. "You will listen to me now and you will get in the car and we will talk about this later. Do you hear?" She turned to Dr. Frost. "You are not welcome to come to my house anymore without calling. And you may never *ever* take Ann like that again. *Do you understand?*"

"Mom, it's okay," I cried. "It's okay."

"Don't worry," Dr. Frost called to me. "We'll work this thing out, don't you worry!"

"Stop brainwashing her!" my mother screamed.

"You're going to be sorry!" Dr. Frost yelled.

"Get in the car," Mom said.

"Wait," I said.

"Get in the car!"

"You haven't seen the last of me," Dr. Frost cried. "Ann and I are going to Japan together next year. Don't you forget it!"

Mom shoved me into her VW Bug, and we took off down the driveway as if making a getaway in a movie. The tires screeched. I held on to the little handle on the dashboard and tried to wave goodbye, but my mother actually slapped down my hand. She drove like that all the way out of the oaks and the narrow canyon, past the big houses and driveways, until we reached the lake and the golf course near the entrance to Hope Ranch. Then she started gasping and breathing as if she'd been underwater. Her face was red and welty. She glanced back and forth in the rearview mirror, as if Dr. Frost might be chasing us down.

Finally she coughed, "Do you understand what happened? Did you know she didn't ask me if you could come up here yesterday?"

I shook my head.

"I found a note on the front door: *Picked up Ann at school, will call later.* I tried calling my father. He was out of town. No one had any idea where she'd gone. I had to go break into their house last night, and I just happened to find the number of a moving company near the phone. But of course they were closed. I had to wait until this morning to find out where the house was. I was awake all night. I've been crying my eyes out!"

"Oh," I said.

"That's right, oh. Are you sure you understand? She kidnapped you! She's out of her mind. This is the first time I've stood up to her in my whole life. Do you see what I've had to live with?" Mom was chewing so hard on her lower lip it was bleeding. She was bending her thumb and pushing the thumb knuckle into her lower lip. She chewed big round circles into her lip that would form soft scabs. "So long as you understand what happened."

"I do, I guess."

"I'll never forget the time she chased our neighbor out of the house with a hammer, just because he asked permission to trim a tree on the property line. She's insane!"

"She and Granddad are finished," I said.

"Yes, I was going to tell you about that," Mom said.

"Well, you don't need to," I said.

Mom looked at me. The little engine roared. "What did she say?"

"Anyway, where's Granddad right now?"

"Fishing trip," Mom said.

"In Denver, Colorado?"

"What difference does it make?" she said.

"Do I have to go to Japan with her?"

"Absolutely not," Mom said. "As if I don't even exist, as if we don't have a family and a life—"

"What if I *want* to go to Japan with her?"

Mom froze. "Haven't you heard anything I've told you?"

"I guess."

"Then why would you ask that?" Shaking the wheel like she was strangling it, about to bite her lips off. "What were you thinking when you drew on her wall?"

"I couldn't sleep," I said.

"So you defaced the wall?"

"No!"

"You drew on a wall. Are you saying that wasn't wrong?"

"Did you even *look* at it?"

"I want you to tell me right now," Mom choked, "that you understand it was wrong!"

"Dr. Frost liked it," I said. "She said people would be studying it for years."

"Oh, my God, what am I dealing with?" Mom cried.

Tears began to flow down her face, as we motored down the highway.

"Mom?" I said, after a while. "Are you okay?"

"I've been better."

"Can we stop and get something to eat?" I said. "I'm really hungry."

"No, I just want to get home."

"All I've had since yesterday is an orange," I said.

"You can wait," she said.

"Can't we go back, and you two apologize?"

"What for?" my mother said. "I didn't do anything!"

"I know, but—"

"We can't go back."

"Are you sure?"

"Be quiet and watch the road!"

I wish I'd said something like, If you don't make up now, you won't speak to each other again until I drag you together on a quiet Tuesday morning near the end of the century, which is a very long time from now. But I didn't know that then, of course. Instead, I said something like, "Look at this neat thing I got for Kathy," and pulled a small screaming head from the pocket of my clothes.

Life on Comet

It's the first time we've been invited to a barbecue, a real barbecue with corn and steaks and lemonade, my whole family together with people from our neighborhood, and over in one corner of the yard, up in a leafy mulberry tree, our bare legs hanging down like exotic gourds, Leslie Foote is testing me on the solar system. We've been studying the planets at school.

"And Comet," she says.

"No, there's only nine."

"You forgot Comet," Leslie says. "It's the smallest."

"There is no planet called Comet."

"Let's ask my dad," she says.

We swing from the branches, drop to the grass, and bound over to the adults, who are clustered under a bamboo trellis to keep from the valley's grinding light. Bowls on the patio table brim with nuts and dips and sturdy chunks of cheese skewered on toothpicks. Mom is holding Kathy on her lap like a shield.

"Hey, everyone," I say. "So, there's no planet called Comet, right?"

Leslie elbows through to her father, the party's host, Mr. Foote. "Dad, tell her, there is!"

"What, doll?" Mr. Foote, insurance adjuster, former football star at USC, all-around-daddiest of the neighborhood dads, wraps his arm around her. His public concern over her knitted brow creates a stab of envy in me I don't really understand. After all, Mom's already convinced me the Footes are boring and stupid and "bourgeois" in a way that ensures we'll never connect with them on any level.

I see Leslie's brow too, but I know it's a ploy. I say, "I'm just trying to explain there's no planet called Comet."

Roy says, "That's right, Ann. A comet is a fragile chunk of matter moving through space."

A bloodcurdling yell rises from the gullet of Leslie Foote, the girl who reveals her beauty secrets to me, like how she brushes her hair a hundred strokes a night, sleeps with a stocking on her head, and uses Prell. *"Comet's the smallest!"* she screams.

Mr. Foote shrugs and sends Roy a sporty wink, directing him out for the pass. "Yes, all right, and then there's little Comet. Right, Weeks?"

Roy glances around the table at the faces of our neighbors, settles last on Leslie, then manages a sickly smile. "Yes, right, little Comet. Of course."

"Told you!" Leslie says. I gape at Roy, and Roy forwards the wink on to me.

"No way," I say.

"Here's to Comet!" our neighbor Mrs. Lewis says, raising her martini.

"To the first man on Comet!" Mr. Lewis chimes in.

"Roy," I cry out, "come on, tell her the truth!"

Then Leslie laughs and says, "Why do you call him Roy?" and I suddenly feel like I'm going to burn up. Doesn't she know Roy's my stepfather?

"Hey, *Howie,*" she yells to Mr. Foote.

"Move," I say.

"You move!"

Now we're in a pushing match. I make ground, then she takes it back, but she's got linebacker blood. She's going to ram me into the house.

"Break it up," Mr. Foote says.

"Stop it!" Mom says, wrestling me from the grip of Leslie Foote. I shrug her away. "I think we'd better go home," she says.

Kathy starts to cry, trembling on the bricks in her best shorts with sunflowers on them. "No, I want to be at the barbecue!"

"Helen, have a seat," Roy says. "It's just kids."

"I'm suddenly not feeling well," Mom says.

I don't want this to happen. No. It can't. I hastily dry my palms on my sides. "We're having a good time, Mom, it's okay."

"I'm sorry, I'm just not feeling well," she says.

"No, it's because of this, isn't it?"

"We're going home now," Mom says.

"Oh, well, nice visiting with you all," Roy says, getting up.

"Seriously?" says Mr. Foote.

My mother has already bolted, out of the Footes' back-yard, down their ivy-fringed driveway, up our elm-shaded street, Kathy calling "Wait!" and galloping to keep up with her. Roy and I amble down the block, doing our worried little walks. The moment we enter our house and close the door, Mom yells at Roy, "Why did you let that monstrous little girl bully you into agreeing there is a planet called Comet?"

"For crying out loud," Roy says. "I thought you wanted to make friends with the neighbors."

"Do we have to pretend we're idiots to fit in around here?"

"No one thought I *believed* it!" Roy says.

"You embarrassed Ann," Mom says. "You embarrassed *me*!"

"So this is *my* fault?" Roy says.

"Stop making such a big deal!" I hear myself yelling at Mom.

"Don't yell at your mother!" Roy yells.

"Don't yell at Ann!" Mom yells at Roy.

"Stop . . . making . . . everyone . . . *mad*," Kathy cries, hitting me with a pillow.

●

It's all too much. I run outside and smash the tetherball around the pole in the driveway, over and over until my knuckles burn, then pace the fence. Late afternoon, Indian summer, the sun wilting the world, my sneakers leaving a stampede of prints in the perishing grass. It's probably over 100. Smog covers the sky like a gray glove, and sometimes, when you breathe hard, it hurts. My chest feels heavy today. I edge my way back inside through the sliding door and find the house quiet, except for the sound of Roy flipping through a newspaper in the kitchen and, as I tiptoe down the hall, the intermittent sniffling of Kathy rocking in a chair.

Mom's door is shut tight. She loves to pull the blinds and crawl into bed. And all of us in limbo until she comes out again.

In my room, the sun burns through the peachless peach tree, and I stomp over a purple throw rug that slips until I've worked it under the bed. Who needs it? I don't like my throw rug, matted and full of burrs. And who cares if Roy's not my "real" father. What's so bad about that?

There IS such a planet as Comet, and we're the only ones on it.

Kathy nudges my door. She's four, has strong square toes she can walk on the tips of, and always wants to pretend she's something else. Like, *I'll be the refrigerator, you be the stove!* or any kind of animal, even weird, unappealing ones, like chuckwallas and musk oxen. "Let's be frogs," is all she asks today.

"I don't want to."

She hops over and grabs my leg.

"Go play frogs with Roy," I say, kicking her.

She jumps on me. "I want to be frogs with *you.*"

I fall back on my bed. I'm tired, very tired. I haven't been sleeping well. Last week we hit on the idea of rearranging my room: the bed against the wall, not sticking out into the room *exposed,* where killers can come at you from both sides. But it's still not quite right. I'm often up roaming the house, knocking things over, and sometimes Mom has to tuck me back in, or bring me milk and pat my head, and I hear them saying maybe something is wrong, *maybe something's bothering her.*

"Want to make things fall into hot lava?" Kathy says.

I groan. "I guess."

"I love that game!" says Kathy, running off to collect the supplies.

My room looks so innocent by day. Just a regular room painted pastel green, with white curtains and a big corkboard on one wall so I can pin things up. On it I've got flower-power stickers and *MAD* magazine covers and John/Paul/George/Ringo and anything psychedelic I can cut out of magazines. And then there's my bureau, and my bookcase, and my desk. It's just right for me. Just about all I could possibly want in a bedroom. But I've fallen prey lately to so many bad dreams (people chasing me down halls, shooting through walls, and then suddenly the inside of a meat locker, full of horrible-looking sausages and flesh) that Mom finally took me to see Dr. Todd, esteemed pediatrician, who prescribed a bitter green syrup with a sedative in it. I can't swallow it. I clench my jaw and it oozes out of my teeth.

(While we're talking about my dreams, about how I'm gloomy and combative, and about displacing those feelings onto my pillow instead of my loved ones, I notice a family portrait on his desk. Dr. Todd and wife and four kids. Puffy-cheeked and greedy-eyed. Yet because they're his, Dr. Todd displays them with pride. *We are the amazing family of Dr. Todd!* is what these ugly kids seem to be bursting with. *Us! The family of Dr. Todd! Wherever we go it's great! Wherever we are, it's the best!* I want to stomp on the family portrait. I want Dr. Todd to tear off his mask and confess they're a band of materialistic gluttons, and that he wakes every morning praying for a new life. But no. We have to talk about *me*.)

Kathy returns, her T-shirt rolled up around a load of victims. We build a huge volcano out of socks. One by one, we drop plastic animals and people into the center. I start to enjoy it. As they fall, we shout out their last words to the world.

"Oh, dear God, forgive me!" I cry, letting go of a duck, and Kathy giggles intensely.

"Why?" She laughs. "What did the duck do?"

Dr. Todd would say I'm *displacing guilt* onto the duck. Last week at school, new year, and there I am stumbling into the girls' bathroom in time to discover some of the older girls wadding up paper and stuffing it into the toilets. Looks fun, so I join in. I'm grabbing paper hand over fist, flushing and stuffing, and at last I manage to create a wad that throws the toilet into cardiac arrest. It sucks and gasps and finally lets out one final burble. The next flush pours water over the top. "Way to go!" says one of them, giving me the nod and fleeing. I feel competent, a success. I leave wet footprints all the way back to class. But someone follows my tracks, and next thing I know I'm on my way to the principal's. Miss Wrist.

"Now what? Last week five girls came into class after recess with their hair lathered up in shampoo. You were the ringleader."

"Mrs. Hagman said her class last year was Head and Shoulders better than us. We were protesting!"

When I arrive home that afternoon, Mom opens the door and says, "Why?" Now I know we'll never go to the back-to-school sales and get the white vinyl boots everyone's wearing. I want them more than I've ever wanted anything. Mom says no, partly because of my misdeed, but also because the feet can't *breathe*. I want to go shopping at real stores, but we never do; no matter how much I squirm and stand lopsided, my mother measures me and makes my clothes instead. They're made out of strange fabrics and buttons she's been collecting for years, and they hang on me like sandwich boards. Luckily my friends think I wear them to be funny.

Not everything's funny. I cry when something unfair happens, like when Mom suddenly gets mad and disappears into her room.

And even when I'm mad at her, I'm always ready to cry thinking that someday, somewhere, Mom might not be alive. For some reason, I'm more afraid of that than anything.

Later, no sign of Mom, Kathy settled down in front of our black-and-white Zenith with a plum, and I have an idea. I take a pack of matches outside with some Oscar Mayer weiners. Half-burned coals line the bottom of the barbecue from the last time we cooked outside, and I attempt to light them. There must be a secret to it. I'm holding the matches until they singe my fingertips, winging them last second into the grass. It's then I notice Roy staring at me from the back porch.

"What are you doing?" he calls.

"Trying to make a barbecue."

He says what he's required to: "You shouldn't be playing with matches."

"Well, they're all gone now," I tell him.

Roy doesn't often get mad. I remember how much I tried to hate him, but he's really not very hatable. Last year he sent my school picture to his mother (not just a wallet-sized one but one of the big ones!), which made me feel so good, when I learned of it, I had to turn my face to the wall.

He crosses the yard now and inspects my work. "Not a bad idea," he says. "What do you say we bring out some fresh charcoal and lighter fluid?"

"Sure."

"We've got ketchup and mustard, relish, the rest?"

"Yeah, I checked," I tell him.

"What should we make for a side course?"

"We have potato chips," I say.

"Okay, we're set," he says. "Come on."

I follow him into our garage, which has never been used to park a car in. It's full of boxes and furniture and tools. "Disaster area," he says, rooting around. "Never find what I'm looking for." He always says this, every time he ventures in there. He shoves boxes aside, tries to lift the lawn mower out of the way. He kicks over a bag of steer manure and hangs a rake on a nail. He cleaves a space between two old dressers full of fossils and rocks. "Bunch of pack rats," he mutters.

Mom has a little area in the corner for projects. She has a pink Formica table, our kitchen table from the old days, and on it is a wooden box filled with different kinds of scissors and supplies. For some reason she really loves scissors. You can't even touch her scissors, she thinks they're so great. On the wall is a bulletin board rustling with articles about newly discovered perils in the world, such as pesticide levels in farmed salmon and botulism in dimpled cans. Today there's something there I've never noticed before. It's a hard little suitcase, and I lift the latches. Inside, fitting perfectly, is a small blue typewriter, so compact it looks like a toy. Smith Corona. I take a piece of paper and roll it in crookedly. I start trying to type.

"What in God's name is this?" Roy says, holding up a big green bubble of melted glass and wire that my mother found once at the scene of a fire.

I say, "I think Mom wants to make something out of that." Then I add, "If she ever comes out of her cave."

It's not our code to mention Mom's cave, and it stops Roy cold in his tracks. "Listen here," he says. "Your mother is a very special person. A very sensitive person, and things get to her in a way that they might not get to you or me. And when that happens, she needs to relax and recover."

"Right." He wants me to understand, be compassionate, rise above it all like a saint. Or maybe he's mad, I can't tell.

"And she's had a very hard time, and even though she doesn't talk much about it, we need to remember what she's been through with that mother of hers," says Roy.

"Yeah, I know."

"Okay. Good girl. Now, let's find that charcoal."

I've been nervously poking at the typewriter. The keys have been overlapping and striking one on top of the other, smudging or missing. Now they're stuck together in a wad, and I reach in and try to pull them apart. My fingers are mottled with ink.

"Can you come here a second?" He's rummaging still. "Roy?"

He says, "I'm busy! What is it now?"

"I just need you," I say.

He stops and regards me, and he's hot and sweaty, but he makes his way over, straddling and shoving as he comes. "What now?" he asks, and when I point at the tangle in the typewriter, he takes the chair and digs in and quickly restores the machine to a usable state. Then he leans forward and straightens the piece of paper and types this:

NOW IS THE TIME FOR ALL GOOD MEN TO COME
TO THE AID OF THEIR PARTY.

"What's that mean?"

"Just habit," Roy says. "Some kind of political slogan from the turn of the century."

He's just warming up. He types some other things then. Part of the Gettysburg Address, then some verse like *Double double, toil and trouble, fire burn and cauldron bubble,* then *I am the captain of the Pinafore, and a right good captain too, I'm very very good, and be it understood*—He's making the little typewriter come alive, every finger flying and the carriage riding out to the side, ringing the bell, and then getting slapped back into place, all in one motion so he doesn't ever have to stop. "What should I type now?" he asks me. "Anything!"

"How about the names of all the teachers at my school?"

"Okay, call 'em out," he says, and I do, and into the typewriter they go by way of his madly octopoidal fingers. Then I start shouting out really goofy things I make up right then, and he types those too. Things like *We are the cows, we are the best, we're getting numerous, we will infest!* By the time he stops, he's almost filled the whole piece of paper, single space. The paper is punctured and bumpy.

"My top speed was one hundred thirty words a minute," Roy says. "I was in the army, but I was stuck in an office."

"Oh," I say, and nod eagerly. My pigtails flop against my shoulders like paintbrushes.

"I've got a lot to learn," Roy says to me. "You know that. I'm not perfect. Not even close!"

I smile and nod some more.

"Well, better find the charcoal and get it going," he says. "This will cheer up your sister. Maybe even your mother."

"And me too," I say.

"And you too," says Roy. "Go in and talk to her, will you? See what you can do?"

This type of assignment makes me feel like I possess the key to our family's happiness, so I head straight inside while Roy fires up the grill. In the garden, near the faucet for the hose, I pass the bed of gray rocks that look like brains. They get wet whenever we water the yard because the faucet drips on them. Mom collected them in Utah. When I was younger and we lived in Long Beach, Mom had the rocks next to our steps there, too. I remember looking at them and thinking how great they were, and saying to Mom, When I grow up I want to be a geologist, just like you. And Mom said, Silly girl, you don't have to be what I am, you know. And I remember that I said, in terrific confusion, *I don't?*

We have some things to be proud of here. In our dining room is a bowl, and in the bowl are some orange petrified disks Mom calls *crinoids*. Crinoids are a life form that took over the world in the Paleozoic era, and Mom used to collect petrified bits of them, all over the Southwest. She has hundreds of pieces of crinoid stems but has never found a prized crinoid *head*. I like grabbing handfuls of them and rattling them like dice, which makes Mom say, "Stop shaking my crinoids!" which is funny.

In our kitchen, in the pantry, are about ten paint-can-sized containers of liquid cane syrup, which my grandmother Dr. Frost used to send us every year for Christmas. She likes doing things like boiling cane and making syrup in her spare time, but she doesn't send it anymore. Not since the falling out, two years ago and counting. Every so often, Mom pries open a can with a screwdriver and harvests the sugar crystals that form continually near the lid. The crystals are in a clump the size of a piece of candy, and we sit on the cool kitchen floor and hold the sticky crystals and chew them up. Then we seal up the cans for next time, and sometimes, when she's doing this, she seems very sad.

"Mom?" I whisper, at her door.

"Come in," she says. This is a good sign: she's talking!

It's dark because the blinds are old and yellowy, and her green blanket covers her like sod. Except for the Seth Thomas clock humming on the nightstand, it's a silent world, away from our neighborhood and every little clang outside. Once, when Mom was upset and I was sent in on a mission like this, I found her staring at the ceiling in a way that made me think, for a moment, she wasn't breathing anymore. I said, "Mom?" and she didn't answer. I really overreacted. I heard a roar in my ears like a waterfall and fainted onto the floor.

Today she pats the bed on Roy's side. I climb up and lay my head on his pillow.

"What's going on out there?" she mumbles.

"We're making a barbecue," I tell her.

"Do we have anything?"

"Hot dogs."

"Don't ever eat them while rooting for a team at a baseball game," she says. "I knew a boy who choked on one and died."

"I know."

On my mother's nightstand is a moth-eaten buff-colored Steiff lion cub that Dr. Frost gave her when she was a girl, which Mom uses now as a pincushion. Full of pins and needles from head to tail, it makes me mad every time I see it. I say, "Hey, is today the day I can pull out the pins?"

She rolls over and looks at it. "What should I use instead?"

I don't think animals should be used as pincushions, even Kathy's blind animals. For some reason she always pulls the eyes off every animal she gets. All these creatures with empty sockets or scabby old glue where the eyes should be.

"Don't we have a *real* pincushion?"

"Probably," Mom says. "I don't know why I started that."

She's warming up, so I'm quick to say, "Sorry about that thing last week."

"What thing?"

"The thing at school."

"Mmm," she says. "Good. I was hoping you'd regret it."

"I do."

"I was hoping you weren't embarking on a life of crime."

"I'm probably not," I say.

"But what an old battle-ax!" she says.

"Yeah!" I laugh.

"And is that her real name?" Mom says. "*Wrist?* What kind of name is that?"

I'm laughing really hard now. "She's a creep!" I scream. "A creepy old wrist!"

Suddenly, Mom frowns. I've noticed this before. The happier I become, the faster her good humor drains away. "What, is Roy doing all the work out there alone?"

"No, it's almost ready." Then I say, "Mom, do you think Roy wants people to think he's not my stepfather?"

"What do you mean?"

"I mean, do you think he wants them to think he's my father?"

"He doesn't care what people think. What are you getting at?"

"I'm just saying, should I be telling people he's not, so they don't think it?"

"Why wouldn't you want them to think it?"

I feel confused now. "I don't mind if they think it, I'm just wondering if *Roy* wants them to think it."

"I'm not going to live my life trapped by what anyone in this neighborhood thinks about *anything*!" Mom says. "Now come on, up up up," she says, as if she's been the one tending to me.

●

A barbecue it is. The hot dogs grilled with black stripes, just right. Mom up and going, her regular self, our queen. Kathy leapfrogging all over the grass. "Look!" she calls. "I'm on a lily pad, look!" We play catch after dinner with a red rubber ball, which Mom likes to see. "I'm so happy you girls have each other," Mom often says. I see my little sister across the yard, trying to catch the ball as if her life depends on it, and wonder if she's actually having fun. I like it better when we're not trying to prove our sisterliness. But the twilight lingers until late, the crickets chirp merrily, and the smell of other barbecues in the neighborhood doesn't rip us in two with loneliness, at least not tonight.

That fall, the Footes start the construction of an addition to their house: a family room in every sense of the word. For Mr. and Mrs. Foote, there will be a wet bar. For Mr. Foote, there will be an enormous closet, with special racks and fixtures to hold his various pieces of sports equipment. For Mrs. Foote, rather than the rickety card tables of yore, there will be a big glass table for her jigsaw puzzles and bridge games. Plus a built-in sewing table and ironing board, a window seat with a telephone, a toy chest, a flagstone fireplace, and a huge console color TV.

It takes four months for everything to be completed, from the pouring of the foundation to the first drinks poured at the bar. I'm over there, playing with Leslie and some other kids, the day they christen the new room. They're having a spontaneous little party. Neighbors are popping in, bringing bottles of Beefeater and Gilbey's and Johnnie Walker to stock the new bar. Mr. Foote takes me aside and says, "Why don't you bring your folks over for a look?"

"Yeah, okay, great!" I say, and run eagerly down the street to tell them about it.

Mom and Roy are raking and weeding in back; Kathy's burying toys in her sandbox. "Guess what?" I say. "The Footes want us all to come over to see their new room!"

Mom doesn't look happy at all. Her face knots up, and she begins to pantomime a child throwing a tantrum, hideously shrieking *"Comet! Comet! Comet!"* and storming up and down. Roy bellows with laughter.

It's kind of funny, but I say, "You know what, I've gotten to know her better, and she's really pretty nice."

The winter sun is going down directly behind them, and Roy moves into my mother's shadow. For a moment I can't see either of them, just one big uppity blob countering my hopes and dreams. "Tell them we'd love to, some other time," it says.

"You're not going to come?"

"Well, it's very nice, but we're busy."

"You're not that busy. Roy, don't you want to?"

He pauses a second, then says, "No, I think not." And then I understand, finally. How Roy's main job, no matter how nice he'll ever be to me, is to stand by Mom. That's what Mom wants, *after all she's been through*. That's why she picked him.

"Oh, please, come on, it'll be fun—remember how we had to leave last time? Everybody's over there, there's food and all kinds of stuff!" I can't believe I'm struggling to hold back a sob over this. It's climbing up into my nose.

"Drop it," Mom says.

"We *need* to go. Come on, please! *Please!*"

"If you mention it one more time, you're going to your room!" Mom shouts.

I feel awful my mother's so mad at me, awful that Roy can't disagree, and, after getting a grip on myself, make the passage back up my street. Every house I walk by contains a different package of people, like presents we could be opening but never do, and I know all their names and play in their yards, but it's always just *me,* and I feel too measly and insignificant to pull it off alone all the time. I want some backup. But at least the air is crisp and clear today, and the mountains we can't see the rest of the year rise up purple and handsome over our valley, and all the front gardens and walkways glow with flowers and berries in the twilight. I really like this neighborhood. I don't want the Footes to get the wrong idea.

So as I approach, I brighten up. I take some deep breaths and relax my face into a smile. And I make my entrance, looking for the biggest person in the room: Mr. Foote. He's standing in front of a roaring fire holding a frosty mug of ale.

"Annie, what can I getcha?" he says, when he notices me.

"Thanks for inviting my parents," I tell him. "They're in the middle of a huge project in our backyard, and they'd love to join in, but you know how it is, and they told me to bring you *this*," I say, lifting up a bottle of vermouth I grabbed from the kitchen cupboard.

Mr. Foote examines the dusty green bottle a moment, and it suddenly occurs to me it's not really nice enough to be a gift. The label's old and wrinkly, and come to think of it, the bottle's only half full. I think Mom used some for cooking chicken.

"Well, thanks much," Mr. Foote says, and gives me a solid pat on the back. "You're welcome around here anytime."

"Oh, good, thank you."

"Now get yourself out back and onto one of those teams!" he commands.

"Right!" I make it my business to look as enterprising as possible, a team player, someone you can count on, someone who never lets you down, and I weave my way out through my neighbors, a whole roomful of them, even ones from around the corners and other streets nearby, all of us citizens of this moment, unanimous in our desire to lift our glasses to the Footes' new room.

We Know Where We Are, But Not Why

During the . . . summer season, 27 employees and 35 overnight guests at Grand Canyon, Arizona, acquired febrile illnesses compatible with relapsing fever. Sixteen cases were confirmed by finding Borrelia spirochetes in peripheral blood smears or inoculated Swiss mice. Acquisition of illness was significantly associated with persons sleeping in rustic log cabins and acquiring bites of "unknown" insects. From rodent nesting materials found in the walls and attics of cabins where cases had occurred, infective *Ornithodoros hermsi* ticks were recovered. This outbreak, the largest yet identified in North America, establishes the North Rim as an endemic source of tick-borne relapsing fever.

—*American Journal of Epidemiology*

What are you doing this summer?" I asked my friend Raoul, one spring day at lunch as we paced the perimeter of the schoolyard.

"Committing suicide," he said.

"Oh," I said. "What else?"

"Probably helping my mother around the house," he added.

"What a drag," I said.

"She speaks in monosyllables and has no idea what's going on in the world, but she's otherwise pretty decent."

We stopped and lit cigarettes, at the farthest point from the gym. "I'm like my mother's guinea pig," I told him.

"Why?"

"I've told you already about our summer plans. It's like she's set up an experiment and wants to see what it does to me."

We were putting our hands through the chain-link fence, sticking our lips out through the openings, so that officially speaking we weren't smoking in the schoolyard.

Raoul said, "Did you know, in Spanish, we call them little rabbits of India?"

"What?"

"Guinea pigs. *Conejillos de Indias.*"

"That means guinea pigs?"

"That's what I'm telling you."

"There's no direct translation of *guinea* or *pig*?"

"Nope."

"Wow," I said. "Instead of stupid, experimental drones—" I looked back. I could see Mr. Poplick, the English teacher, who had mentioned the word *orgasm* almost every day since the beginning of the year, coming across the grass toward us.

"Yes," he said. "We imbue them with a certain exoticism."

We flicked our butts into the street outside the fence, dug our hands into our pockets, and turned to face Poplick, who would snidely cut us down for favoring tobacco over marijuana. How could something be a pig in one place and an exotic little bunny in another? It made me wonder what I could be, if I ever had the chance to switch worlds.

●

It was the year I turned sixteen, the year my mother, who had been for some time housebound in the smallest world she could fashion for herself, suddenly accomplished an amazing feat. She decided to be cheerful—all the time, no matter what. "I use self-discipline to pick you up from school on time and make dinner every night," she said. "Why shouldn't I make myself be happy?"

In the fall she enrolled in some extension classes at UCLA, which loosened her up about driving to a destination, getting out, and interacting with people. But her breakthrough came when she found a part-time job at a special backpacking store in Glendale, not just a shop but a *hub,* a center for wilderness types, a place where activists posted flyers and meetings were held and talks were given and she was there in the thick of it, selling boots and moleskin and providing tips on which dehydrated foods tasted best and pouring over USGS maps with hikers and dispensing her knowledge of river trips and trails. She was a hit there, and she liked it. I was happy for her. But somehow this led her to apply for a summer job as a ranger at a certain national park, and—calling upon some contacts from the old days, including some higher-ups in the Park Service and the Sierra Club—she got the job. *An actual ranger.* She'd have a ranger car, wear a ranger outfit, give nature talks, lead nature walks. Truly grotesque.

"We get our own cabin in the compound," Mom was saying. She was losing weight to fit into the uniform, giddy over her accomplishment. "No way on earth are you staying home. You and Kathy can roam and play."

"But I was planning to hang around with my friends and maybe go to Tahoe with Susie's family," I said.

"Don't be so shortsighted," she said. "You can do that any summer."

"No, I can't," I said. "It's probably the only summer I'll *ever* be able to do that."

"You depend too much on your friends," she said.

"What about you?"

Mom said, "It's time I met some people of substance."

My mother had an assortment of new friends from the backpacking store. River rafters and oarsmen, with names like Connie Bohn and Spencer Chang and Ned Martinez. Hikers like Lewis Blaustein and Dena Fladeboe. Independently wealthy adventurers like Angus Frey. They were coming by our house all of a sudden, and Mom and Roy were having raucous dinner parties, and Kathy and I would clean up in the kitchen while they hooted out in the living room, pretending we were hunchbacked scullery maids in a manor house, scraping the plates and hand-washing the good silver, then stabbing it away in its felty sleeves.

Angus Frey was an Australian, a man with a head the size of a bull's, a rumpled, bulbous face, thick dark hair like a pelt, and a voice used to speaking to crowds, a man who tossed laughs from his chest like bricks and spent his time traveling and doing good deeds, such as protesting new dams in the Sudan or spreading the word about endangered species in the Amazon, or about timbering, or littering, or oil drilling: you name it. He'd written books on his exploits. He talked up a storm, words hammering on everything within his range. Spokesman for a group founded in Sydney, he roamed the world, but somehow, lately, here he was in our living room.

"Listen here, girls, do you know the story of Truganini?"

"No," we said. We crowded at his enormous feet.

"Before the settlers came to Tasmania, it was peopled by a race which had lived there for thousands of years. And of course when the British arrived in 1803 they had to clear the slate, and they killed these people off by the thousands. Truganini was the last woman of her kind. She lived a government-subsidized life and was subject to all manner of unwanted exposure, and one of her greatest fears was what would become of her remains after she died. Promises, promises. Sure enough, they strung up the woman's bones in a museum in Hobart."

"Is that good or bad?" said Kathy.

"Bad," said Angus Frey.

"Aren't you slanting it, by using the words *strung up*?" I

said. "If you'd said *commemorated* or *protected* the story'd have a whole different twist."

"My word, yes, you've got me, I'm a propagandist at heart," he said. "But you see, no matter how you say it, it was a tragedy."

"Indeed it was," agreed Roy.

"The girls have been very moved by the plight of the American Indian," Mom threw in.

"We have?" I said.

"Your favorite book is *Island of the Blue Dolphins*," Mom said.

"Are you kidding?" I said. "Not for a long time. My favorite book is *Das Kapital*."

"That's right, I keep forgetting you're an intellectual now."

"My favorite book is *Little House on the Prairie*," said Kathy.

"I also greatly relish the works of Kafka and Dostoevsky," I added.

"As well you should," Angus Frey said.

"All right, girls, say good night," Mom said.

"I want to ask something," Kathy said, standing on her toes.

"Yes?" Mom said.

"I want to ask *him*."

"Ask away," Angus Frey said.

"Your sister was eaten by a shark?" she said, obviously hoping it was true.

Mom blanched. "I'm sorry, Angus. Please go to bed now, both of you."

"It's all right," said Angus Frey. "Happened long ago. Don't fret over it, I've made my peace. I often tell people about the rough water down our way, teeming with life, with so much to offer and just as much to take away."

"You shouldn't mention things like that to people," Roy said to her while we were brushing our teeth.

"Why?"

"Because it's probably a very painful memory."

"Sorry," said Kathy.

"No, really, I hope you understand. It's similar to the way we don't talk about your mother's mother, because it hurts her," Roy said.

"But I think we *should* talk about her," I said.

"It's not really up to you," Roy said.

"I knew her too, doesn't that mean anything?"

"Mama doesn't like it when you talk about her," Kathy said.

"You didn't even know her," I said.

"All right," Roy said. "Pajamas."

"I'm spitting," Kathy said.

"After spitting." Roy sighed.

And then it was June, the night before our trip. I had plans. I tore off on my bike after dinner to meet up with Raoul because we were invited to a party at Mindy's, and as soon as I started to move of my own accord, I felt somewhat less depressed. Warm air rose from the pavement in waves, gusting up my arms, fanning my face with twilight. I knew these streets down to the different grades of asphalt they'd been surfaced with, recognized like geological formations every bump and crack in the road. I also spent a lot of time inspecting the ways people tried to make their properties distinctive, with flags, or eagles over the doors, or special mailboxes, or pudgy mounds in the middle of their lawns appointed with birdbaths and gnomes. I told myself to relax, that I wouldn't miss much. I'd be back soon.

I met Raoul at the designated corner, and we cycled over side by side. By the time we arrived at Mindy's, a small stucco house north of Victory Boulevard, Pat and Randy were making out on the couch, Beth and Mark were making out in an armchair, Louise and Alan were making out on the grass in back, and Carole King's album *Tapestry* was going around and around on the turntable, making Diane cry because Diane still loved Randy.

I picked out a few Doritos from a big bowl, took another look around the darkened living room, and said, "Let's go."

"Me first," said Raoul.

We hopped back on our bikes and rode a few miles over to Pierce. Pierce was an agricultural college then, in the west end of the valley, where the Santa Monica Mountains rolled down to the basin. The air smelled green with alfalfa, and at night it was the best place to ride. The walkways were well-lit, built on gently rolling hills, so you could glide down them and feel like you were flying.

I had a green Nishiki ten-speed. I'd saved all my money, from trimming ivy up and down the block, mowing the lawn every Saturday morning, cleaning the bathroom, and folding laundry, to get it:

Bicycle		$119.95
Tax		$6.00
License		$1.00
Chain		$10.95
Lock		$3.95
Book rack		$4.95
Tax		$.95
TOTAL		$147.75
Roy and Mom's		
contribution:		-$15.00
My savings		-$90.00
BALANCE loaned		
by Mom and Roy:		$42.75
payment	1/25	$2.50
owing		$40.25
payment	2/15	$1.80
owing		$38.45
payment	2/17	$2.25
owing		$36.20
payment	2/18	$15.00
owing		$21.20

payment	2/24	$10.00
owing		$11.20
payment	3/29	$6.00
owing		$5.20
payment	5/29	$5.20
owing		$0.00 !!!

Down went our bikes into the grass, and we sprawled out like earthworms beside them. The grass felt cool and spongy. From under a distant floodlight came the sound of a tennis ball receiving some good sharp whacks.

"You didn't want to stay, did you?" I said.

"No way," said Raoul. "It was like an orgy in there."

"I know it."

"I mean, I like those people, but I just wasn't in the mood."

"Me either," I said.

"It's hard to believe people even have orgies," Raoul said. "I mean, real orgies."

"Yeah," I said. "I, personally, would feel too self-conscious."

"Right. Like, I'm really going to relax and get into making love to someone with ten people watching," Raoul said.

I pressed my lips together and nodded. Somewhere, deep down, I harbored a lot of feeling for Raoul. But I'd never shown it. I wasn't sure he felt the same way. I was afraid that if I reached over and tried to kiss him, it would wreck everything.

Raoul had a little flask of Southern Comfort and he offered it. I took a swig. Then we lit our Marlboros, and I watched a small plane with a green light flying over the valley like a bug. The rest of the sky gray as a parking lot. "I really, *really* don't want to go away," I said.

"Nothing you can do about it?"

"I've argued but it's no use."

"Do you think the song "The Bear Went Over the Mountain" is anti-travel?" Raoul said, tapping a blade of grass against his front teeth.

"How?"

"Well, because all he could see was the other side of the mountain," Raoul said.

"So it's not worth it to go anywhere, is that what you think the song's about?"

"I'm just *wondering* if that's what it's about," he said.

"Maybe it's anti-bear," I said. "Since it's the bear's perceptions, the bear's nearsightedness, the song celebrates."

"Why would a song celebrate a bear's nearsightedness?"

We'd planted ourselves about twenty feet from a pig enclosure, and suddenly, as if there had been a change in the direction of the wind, we could hear the animals snorting in their pens.

"Maybe because as nation builders destroying the wilderness, it was better to think it didn't matter," I suggested.

"I get it," Raoul said. "When ravaging forests, no need to think of the bears, because when they go over the mountain, they appreciate nothing."

"Exactly." I laughed. I thought of telling this to Angus Frey.

"I'm hungry," said Raoul.

We climbed on our bikes again and went whooping down the hill.

Out on the flat, shifting gears, we zipped down Winnetka, and the warm air tickled my neck and my hair waved behind me like a flag. We hugged the corner at Sherman Way, cycled into downtown Reseda, stopped and bought ice cream cones at Sav-On, and sat on the high square curb to eat them.

Reseda. A pornographic bookstore and a sewing and hobby center existed side by side, as did a church and a liquor store. In December someone hung tin dreidels on the wires and ratty candy canes on the streetlights. It was a town and it wasn't. It had an honorary mayor instead of a real one. It was part of LA but it was called Reseda, just like there was Encino and Tarzana and Canoga Park. In a low and dismal appliance store across the street, a double row of televisions flashed a cheesy variety show with some warty old guy in a sequined cape singing his lungs out.

"Don't you think it's kind of disturbing, seeing a bunch of TVs on together like that?" I said.

"Yeah," said Raoul. "As a matter of fact, I do." He was licking his green pistachio ice cream into a square.

"I wonder why."

"Maybe it makes you feel like an insect," he proposed. "You know how flies have those compound eyes?"

"I do."

"The philosopher-psychologist William James writes about how it feels really unpleasant to sit on a warm spot created by someone else. If he can write about that, we can write about this."

"Good idea!"

We were on the staff of the school paper, so the next fall we printed a little blurb about it. We offered a prize to anyone who could tell us why we didn't like the sight of many television sets lined up in a store. Then we printed all the replies, proclaiming the last to be the winner:

- *It's not depressing. It's a sign of a healthy economy, you pinkos.*
- *Since your eyes don't know which one to choose, you feel inadequate and confused.*
- *Decadent consumerism.*
- *It makes you feel like a lot of people except you are going to be getting a new TV.*
- *The normal has become significantly grotesque.*
- *It's a visit to the future when the powers that be mock and control us from a screen.*
- *What a bogus contest, use the space for sports.*

Meanwhile, I was still mulling the question of warm spots on seats, particularly horrible on toilets.

"So, I wrote a new poem," Raoul said then, from our perch on the curb in front of Sav-On.

"Oh?" I said, and felt the corners of my mouth curling into a nervous smile.

"I guess I feel a little weird, just a little, about having you read it. I mean, I say some shit that sounds weird, sort of out of context. And it's sort of in the straight-up thought-stream tradition, because I was trying to let as much slip out as possible. You know, actually, writing this bullshit really helps relieve my frustrations about being stuck in this present reality. I guess I'm ready to show it—sorry for doing so much prefacing—I'm basically a little insecure about my stuff sometimes, but with you I should feel safe."

He pulled a wadded-up piece of paper out of his pocket and handed it to me.

"So, it's called 'Sad Viviana,' " he said.

" 'Sad *Viviana*?' "

Viviana sat in the front of our French class, blond hair reaching for her hips.

After a few seconds, he said, "By the way, I totally want to say I dug that article you wrote about your mother finding a thumb in a soda bottle."

I sniffed.

"Was it true?"

"Who knows? She said it was," I said.

He started to laugh. "Did she sue?"

"Thumbs are probably everywhere," I said. I'd finished my ice cream; my hands were sticky; it was time to take off. "I made a mistake in the tone of that article."

"How?"

"It was just wrong. I glorified my mother instead of questioning her."

"That would have been distracting," Raoul said.

"Well, see you later," I said.

"That's it?"

"Gotta go," I said.

"Hey, are you going to write or what?"

"I'll write."

"You'd better," he said. "Let me know what you think of that poem."

I pedaled away, crossing the cement-bedded, litter-stained, rat-run LA River at Tampa, taking the dark bumpy way down Topham into my neighborhood, the poem festering in my pocket like a dead thing. Maybe I had it wrong, maybe it would say something negative about Viviana. Like that she was a leech upon society. But I doubted it. The poem would surely imply there was something deep about her, something complex and doomed. What about me, though, wasn't I complex and doomed?

I arrived home right as Mom was pulling up in her car from work. She didn't see me in the dark, coasting up to her car. She was curled over, looking intently at something, and upon hearing my voice, she jumped a little.

"Mom."

"Hello, dear," she said. Her hands disposed of whatever she was holding as if she'd performed a magic trick, but I thought I saw a small white box disappear from sight. "Help me carry these bags in. I bought some supplies tonight for our trip, with my discount."

"What were you looking at?"

"Nothing, nothing," Mom said.

"I saw a little box, like for jewelry."

"Oh, that?" She shrugged, pulled the box from her pocket, and opened it for me. On a square of green velvet lay a silver pendant shaped like a woman's head.

"Who is it?"

"It's Truganini. You remember the story," Mom said, snapping shut the lid.

"Is that, did—?"

"Look at this receipt! I bought out the store!" She waved a long tail of paper at me, like a pesty kite.

●

In the morning we were off, my mother and sister and I, climbing into our loaded-down Buick before dawn. Roy stood in the headlights clutching his de-elasticized pajama bottoms in one hand, waving to us with the other. He'd join us later in the summer, as soon as he possibly could.

"Bye!" we cried, driving away.

"See you soon!" Roy faded.

Where were we going? It was a place to which people by the long caravans and busloads rolled out year after year, to take pictures, buy postcards, cross off their lifetime lists. I knew I should have been more enthusiastic, more agreeable, more supportive and glad, but when you hear about this place the rest of the year too, see books lying around about it, have *rare prints* of it all over your house, just how much longing can you drum up?

Anyway, I had other names for it: *Sublime Cleft, Exalted Fissure, Noble Crevice, Overvalued Crack.*

The ice chest squeaked the whole distance. In Barstow, we fueled up at a certain gas station that Mom had claimed for years contained an unattributed mural by Orozco. "I've seen his work at the Dartmouth College library, and I'm certain it's his," she pompously liked to say. The morning sun was shimmering on the concrete, making optical illusions that reflected like glass. Tumbleweeds and dust devils skittered over the crusty ground. The wind carried grit in it, as the earth dried up and flew away.

The Park Service compound turned out to be a cluster of brown cabins next to a parking lot full of gas tanks and government vehicles. Our one-bedroom cabin was stuffy and dilapidated, with old vinyl flooring curling away from the baseboards like unhealthy toenails, revealing a mat of dead insects, dust, and hair. The kitchen smelled like propane, and the bathroom was equipped with flaking fixtures and a shower stall so cramped you knocked your elbows sudsing up. In the living room, Kathy and I slept on canvas cots reminiscent of battlefield stretchers, positioned around a potbellied stove that was rough and corroded and smelled like it had been used to burn human protein in. Forget television. We were lucky to have a lamp. All along the tops of the log walls, pockets of nesting materials—pine needles, newspaper scraps, kapok—dangled and bulged like half-extruded dung.

Behind the cabin sat a big white block of salt, there for the purpose of luring mule deer forth from the woods to lick it, in a bright patch of sunlight coming through the aspen and pine. It worked. Morning and night we saw their thin pink tongues flickering from their black-lipped muzzles, necks craned, frightened of being so close to the cabins but driven by their need to sample the white rock.

"What's wrong with you anyway?" Mom asked me, our second day there.

"Something's been biting me all over."

"Stop sulking," she said. "Get out and take a walk. Try to absorb your surroundings. Isn't it great, being away from that metropolitan morass?"

"It's not that great. I have nothing to do."

"I just told you what to do," she said.

"But I don't want to do that."

"Suit yourself, then, if you want to waste this chance. By the way, did I tell you girls our friend Angus Frey will be visiting sometime soon?"

"I like Angus Frey," said Kathy.

"Where's he going to stay?" I said.

"At the lodge," Mom said. "He won't be in your way, will he?"

"Why is he coming?"

"He's never been. Is that good enough for you?"

"I thought he'd been everywhere," I said.

She said, "Isn't it nice to know you still have so much to learn?"

"Have you called Roy yet? When do we get to talk to him?" I always tried to get the last word with my mother.

She was revising the text of her campfire talk, practicing in front of the mirror in her room. She had a tape recorder, and she was taping herself too. At night she would be delivering these talks in an open-air amphitheater to a surprisingly large and attentive group of people spending the night in the park. After the talk, people would raise their hands and ask questions. Hearing the strange lilt of her voice as she rehearsed, a sort of Vassar/Annie Oakley hybrid, I'd cringe.

I had a lot of books and I sent out letters, and letters began to come in, and I heard long descriptions of parties and sleepovers my friends were having, and sometimes they collaborated on messages to me, and everyone signed. One day I received an envelope from Raoul and was chagrined by how happy it made me to see my name in his handwriting. He wrote, "Did you hear Poplick got canned? Someone told the administration he smoked dope in his spare time, and he wouldn't deny it. I salute the man for his integrity and hope he's having lots of orgasms!"

Too bad. Poplick was a good teacher, creator of haunting vocabulary sentences like *I talked to the homunculus in the supermarket*. I wondered how he was taking it, what he'd do with himself next.

In between waiting for mail, between chapters in books, I walked in the woods. Preferably alone. I could pretend I wasn't there that way. I could live in the world of my next letter to Raoul. I'd try to make it engaging and pithy, just the right blend. One day, in the piebald light of the forest, I noticed a squirrel sitting on a log and decided to join it. Not only did the squirrel hold tight, but after a few minutes of twitching and staring it began to inch my way. I held out my open palm, the way I'd been taught to put strange dogs at ease. The squirrel moved closer and sniffed my hand, and I felt its short rapid breath on my skin. A wild animal was paying attention to me! Its eyes shined like beads of oil; I've always remembered the strange thought I had looking at them. I was trying to define the look of a live eye compared to that of a dead one. *In the difference is the mys-*

tery of love. The squirrel and I sat together awhile; then, with a spasm of its brow, it shot off into a narrow purple shadow between the trees.

●

And so Angus Frey joined us, as announced. Sitting in the kitchen with the low ceiling and hodgepodge of stinks, sipping red wine with Mom from paper cups, he looked improbable there, a schooner in a bottle. He mashed beef Stroganoff up the backside of his fork, using his knife like a pushbroom across the scratched Melamite plates. He asked us questions: Was Kathy obsessed with baseball because of the sport of it or because she could record the statistics? Was I trying to teach myself Russian because I was interested in the culture or because I identified with the country's status as enemy? Did we understand how Parliament worked? Had we heard the latest on Aboriginal land rights, or the nuclear testing in the South Pacific, atolls glowing with waste, and had we tasted kangaroo? Mom put on lipstick for these dinners. She was thirty-six years old.

●

And then came the episode with the tree, and all that followed. I could easily start with how my mother's legs were astride this fallen tree, a log as wide as she could straddle, a Ponderosa pine tall enough to topple from one side of the narrow dirt road and land on the other, fully blocking our way. We had taken a little day trip down an obscure Park Service road, a road to a lookout point, a dead end. And while Mom and Angus Frey discoursed on the geologic panorama before our eyes, a thunderstorm stole over and lightning cracked like whips, sent us sprinting to the car, Mom whooping like a kid, Angus Frey breathing hard, the smell of wet cloth and hair filling the Buick while Mom turned on the engine, the windows steaming, Kathy's teeth chattering the way that usually made me laugh. I rubbed her bare arms like I was trying to coax a fire. I had an awful headache. "Let's light the stove and have cocoa when we get back," Mom said. As we drove along the rough muddy road through the dim light of the forest, the newly fallen log appeared before us like a premature horizon, none of us sure what we were seeing. We stopped and got out and assessed.

"We'll have to get over it somehow," Mom said. "No one will be coming to save us."

We were twenty-five miles from the compound, damp and chilled, and Mom had a talk that evening, and yet she was watching Angus Frey patiently as he attempted to pry at this log, sweat beading on his neck, removing all but his undershirt as he jabbed at it with the crowbar he'd rooted out from the back of the car. "Not making much of a dent, am I?" Angus said to my mother.

"I know what we'll do. We'll collect logs and sticks. We'll stack them along the tree on both sides, and we'll make a ramp and drive over the top of it."

"A bloody good plan," Angus said, shaking the kink from his platter-sized hand.

"I feel crummy," I said.

Mom said, "The sooner we get this thing built, the sooner we'll get back."

Kathy and I were sent into the forest to look for logs and sticks.

"I feel really sick," I told her.

"I feel cold," Kathy replied.

Her upper lip was stiff, the way she looked when she might cry. I said, "Don't worry, there's one."

"It's too big."

"No, just grab it and pull."

"Are we lost?" she asked.

"We know *where* we are," I said. "We just can't get *away* from where we are."

"We're here because a tree fell down," Kathy said.

I said, "Ostensibly."

"So we're lost?"

"I just told you, we're not lost." The branches we pulled up from the floor of the forest were moist, measled with fungus and lichen. As we dragged them along, they splintered apart into pulp.

"So what are we?"

"We're stuck," I said.

"Stuck." She tasted the sound of it. She was eight years old, serious and graceful in a way that made me think she'd be a legitimate human being one day. "Like the animals in the La Brea tar pits?"

"They were stuck in tar. We're not stuck in tar," I said.

"What are we stuck in?"

"Look, isn't it obvious? There's a big thick log across the

road, and we can't drive over it until we build a ramp. You can see that."

"What if we can't build a ramp?" Kathy said.

"I don't know; we'll have to camp here and we'll get hungry and then we'll probably resort to cannibalism," I said.

"Ew," she said.

"We'll make a pact not to eat each other or Mom. We'll eat Angus Frey," I said, suddenly feeling nauseated.

"Come on, you can carry more than that," Mom said, when we chucked the sorry limbs onto the pile.

"Mom, I feel sick."

"Funny how you feel sick now, right when we need your help."

"No, my head feels like there's a knife in it."

"It's the altitude, you're not used to exerting yourself. We're making progress, keep it up." And maybe we were— especially Angus Frey, who could carry two logs at once, like a bear dragging his kill. He'd place his offerings at Mom's feet, and Mom would test the wood with her boots, kicking and stomping it into form. We still needed a lot more to bolster the pile to the necessary height, wide enough for a car.

"We're sticky," said Kathy.

"Stuck," I said.

It started to rain again. The rain tapped through the trees, soft and steady.

"We have some curious specimens of wildlife in Australia," said Angus Frey. "For example, girls, do you know what mother kangaroos are capable of?"

"Oh, about the blastocysts?" Mom said. "That's fascinating. Yes, tell them."

"The female knows when it's a good time to rear her young, and if conditions are poor—say by way of a drought; food's scarce—she can hold on to her fertilized egg in a condition of stasis, or diapause. When conditions improve, the embryo begins to grow again."

My head spun. "You mean," I said, "like now?"

"Like now what?"

"You mean if we were a bunch of pregnant kangaroos, since we're stuck, we'd do this now?"

"If you were starving, yes, I reckon you might," said Angus Frey.

I said, "Why are you talking about pregnant kangaroos?"

"He's telling you something interesting," Mom instructed me.

"How big a setback does it have to be?" I rasped. "I mean, can the kangaroos stop the embryo for an hour because of some little setback like this and then, if everything turns out okay, just start it up again?" Sweat was pouring down my face.

"That I cannot tell you," Angus Frey said. "A fine question, however."

"I don't know if I believe it. It goes against everything we learned in biology."

"Indeed, though some hormone's responsible—"

"Now that I think about it, it's *totally impossible.*"

"Why are you so worked up?" Mom said, staring at me.

"Perhaps she'll be a biologist, and she can come to Australia and research the matter."

"I don't feel right," I said. "Mom?"

"What?"

"I feel horrible."

Out of range of Angus Frey, she lowered her voice to a hiss. I felt her fingernails dig into my wrist. *"I put up with your friends year in and year out, you'd-better-just-this-once-put-up-with-mine."*

"What are you talking about?" I pulled away and wrapped my arms over my chest. The sky was dimming, and another swell of nausea surged through me. "Mom?"

"It's time," she announced, and took the wheel of our family car.

"All clear," Angus Frey called out, and we stood to the side.

The Buick rolled backward twenty feet. Throwing it into DRIVE, she approached the log at a confident pace. The ramp consisted now of many twigs, stumps, and rocks, and some support stakes hammered straight into the rough bed of the road by Angus Frey. The front wheels made contact and began to mount. The pile snapped and groaned but held. The Buick reached the crest. The back wheels began to spin. Mom gunned the engine and rocked her weight onward behind the wheel. Our family vehicle lurched and stopped halfway, suspended over the fallen tree like a see-saw. "Oh, hell!" I heard her say. Yet she wasn't lashing out like she'd usually be doing if I wasn't pulling the lint out of the dryer efficiently, or if Roy were putting the knives away in the wrong drawer. "Come on, then, let's give her a push!" Angus roared, and up we were behind, our palms flat on the rump of the car, shoving and rocking it with all our might. At last the front end tilted forward and the vehicle rolled down the pile on the other side and coasted a few feet before Mom brought it to a halt.

"Beaut!" cried Angus Frey, and as I moved in the direction of the car every muscle in my body contracted, my arms and legs turned to lead, and my throat erupted like a volcano.

"*Unnnh,*" I said.

"Mama, Ann's throwing up!" screamed Kathy.

"Classic," I heard her say. Then Angus Frey was holding my head, swabbing my brow with his hanky. He was lifting me in his arms and carrying me to the car. "Helen, your daughter's burning alive," he said. My mother ran over and tested my face with her cold hands.

She said, "Why didn't you tell me?"

●

"Good evening and welcome. I'd like to introduce myself. I'm Helen Weeks and I'm a ranger naturalist for the National Park Service. I'd like to make one announcement regarding our programs here. We're having a naturalist-accompanied hike tomorrow very early in the morning. . . ."

I could hear Mom practicing from my new world in the back bedroom. A damp washcloth was molded, lukewarm, to my forehead. The new painkillers had codeine in them, and I couldn't keep much food down as of yet. My fever had been spiking at 105. I'd burned and poured sweat and had chills under the blankets that had racked my body with shudders so fierce I'd been afraid I would bite my tongue off. My skull felt like it was being probed by an ice pick. My gums were bleeding. The dryness in my throat was making me gag, and then I'd vomit up some kind of bile. My tongue felt raw. I had an itching rash all over my chest and back and stomach. Light drove pain through my eyes. In the darkness, muted images whirled on the black screen before me, running together like stains. My limbs and joints ached so intensely that tears dampened my face.

The first morning, a Park Service nurse stuck a thermometer under my tongue and told Mom I probably had a case of the flu. Fever blurred the day away. I know Mom came into the room at one point and said, "Some of the other people around the compound seem to be coming down with this, so they've called the Centers for Disease Control in Atlanta, and some men are flying out tomorrow to take blood samples."

"Disease control?"

"I know, who could imagine this," she said, and her cool hands weren't as shocking now on my skin.

The next day, two men came to examine me. I protected my eyes from the light, but through my fingers I could see they were wearing safari outfits. They had a canvas satchel full of equipment and, without much conversation, drew several vials of my blood. I'd never had that done before, but it didn't hurt at all.

"What do you think it is?" I asked them.

"Can't tell you until we examine your sample, but the symptoms are pointing to tick-borne relapsing fever. We'll get you started on antibiotics and give you some stronger pain relief, all right?"

"Thank you," I said, and a few minutes later threw down a handful of pills.

Tick-borne relapsing fever. Mom said it only destroyed the organs when treatment was tardy, and was fatal a mere ten percent of the time. It was caused by spirochetes, nasty spiral-shaped bacteria similar to those responsible for syphilis. Though the antibiotics would kill the first round that had infected me, and I'd start to feel better in a few days, the spirochetes would create clones that would survive and come back to make me sick all over again. And then most likely a few more times before the whole thing ran its course.

"What are you doing today?" I asked my mother, my third day on antibiotics.

"I have a talk out at Cape Royal, and then tonight I'm giving my fireside talk."

"What's Kathy doing?"

"Well, fortunately Angus is keen on taking her on hikes and showing her around. And she likes him."

"Where are they now?"

"They've gone to the lodge to get ice cream."

"Sounds like fun," I said, gloomily.

"They're getting some for you," she added. "Then Roy's coming this weekend."

"That's good," I murmured.

"You don't mind being left in the cabin alone this afternoon, do you?"

"I guess not," I said.

Then she moved out of the room and all was dark again, though I could hear her voice through the walls.

"The oldest exposed rock in the canyon is the Vishnu Schist, a spectacular Precambrian rock, a very hot, dark, volcanic kind of rock, massive and contorted, formed one point eight billion years ago. . . .

"The river has its tools, the boulders, cobbles, sand, silt, and mud, which have taken this great amount of carving in hand. . . . Prior to the closing of the Glen Canyon Dam in 1963, five hundred thousand tons of sediment were transported any given day by the current. But man has permanently altered the process by which this canyon evolved. . . .

"The redwall limestone is actually a grayish-white limestone, dyed by the red beds above, full of iron oxides that wash down when the rains come—"

"How long is it?" I called out.

"How long is the river?" Mom came to the door. "It's about fourteen hundred miles long. Do you need anything?"

"No," I said.

"Am I bothering you?" she said. "I just need to practice a few more minutes."

"Fine," I said, and she closed the door and started up again.

After a few minutes, I yelled out, *"How deep is it?"*

I heard Mom say, "It's often up to seventy feet deep before a rapid, then of course very shallow at a rapid where the water runs over the rocks—"

"Polluted?" I called.

She came to the door. "What is it?" she said. "I don't think you should be shouting like that. You need to rest."

"I'm resting." I wanted her to sit with me, but since she didn't think of it, I didn't ask, and after a while, she left for work.

In the dark room I had become like a blind person, sensitive to the slightest of sounds. I could hear the aspens quake. I could tell when a pine needle plinked on the roof. I even recognized the rough sound of deer lapping at the lick. When I started to feel a bit better, I'd get up in the empty cabin, feel the cold vinyl under my feet, and squint out the windows, amazed at how fast I'd gone from a normal person to an invalid. My legs were shriveled and unsteady. I'd lost nearly ten pounds. My skin was pale as paper, the whites of my eyes thin and gray.

One afternoon I propped myself up and wrote Raoul a letter. I still ached all over, but for the first time in days I felt I could put some cogent thoughts together. It was gratifying trying to describe how sick I'd been, and I hoped he cared. Finally I wrote:

Sorry it's taken me so long to get back to you about "Sad Viviana." It's a great poem. I like the way the point of view shifts halfway through, so that you're never really sure whether it's Viviana who's sad or the narrator. It's clear he's projecting a lot of stuff onto Viviana, and that's definitely the nature of immature attraction. I liked the images of decay and evil that you invoke to show his deteriorating state of mind, and the lengths to which he goes to embroi-

der her shallow simple-minded responses to him. Good work!

It was best to tackle such things head-on.

And the summer proceeded. Angus Frey said goodbye, which was just as well. Roy arrived and played cards with me while I got better, and I was glad he was still there when I had my first relapse. He dug up a little transistor radio for me to listen to at odd hours when I couldn't sleep. In the middle of the night I could get stations as far away as Nebraska and Oklahoma. In the afternoons Kathy would read to me out loud if my eyes were sore; it was funny hearing her peep out an especially hateful and paranoid passage from *Notes from Underground:* " '. . . But in that cold, abominable half-despair, in that conscious burying oneself alive for grief in the underworld, in that hyperconsciousness and yet to some extent doubtful hopelessness of one's position, in that hell of unsatisfied desires turned inward . . .' "

Then, one night, Mom sat on the edge of my bed and said, "You know, I've been meaning to tell you something. I'm sorry I was unsympathetic when you first got sick."

"You mean, the day we were stuck behind the log?" I said.

"Yes. I felt like a real heel. I had no idea. I guess I just thought—well, that you were trying to annoy me."

"Annoy you?"

"You know, try to ruin the mood, because I was having a good time."

"You mean, with Angus Frey?"

"Well, in general."

That was all weeks ago, now, and I was on my third relapse. I'd spent most of my summer in this bed. The view from my pillow was what I'd remember most clearly, that and scattered glimpses of my mother, cheerful all the time now, a picture of health and activity, tanned and slim, her teeth gleaming when she moved like a hungry shark.

"Hey, but Mom," I said, "why would I do a thing like that?"

Let Me Take You Down

I was under the dormitory in the dirt, poking wires from an old black dial phone at a totem pole of lines I'd discovered in an unlocked box attached to the foundation. When the wires brushed certain screws, a blast of static crackled in my ear, but in a moment I found a steady dial tone, so I wrapped the wire tight and placed the call.

"Archie?" I said, when he answered.

"I thought you couldn't call."

"Well, I found a way." The smell of soil and mildew and old asbestos was making me want to sneeze.

"What's new?" he asked.

"Did you get my letters?" I said.

There was a click, heavy breathing.

"I got two. How many'd you send?"

"Who's this?" a voice interrupted. I thought I recognized it as belonging to the oxlike girl from Orinda who frequently boasted about her family's political connections. "Who's on my phone?"

"What's this, a party line?" Archie said.

"Whoever's butting in should hang up," I said.

"This is my phone," the voice complained. "Get off! I'm counting down from ten—"

"My ear is better," I managed to say.

"That's good," Archie said.

"You know, I'm still worried about that bill for the doctor, and then the door."

"Yeah, sorry about that," he said.

"You should help me out," I said.

"Three . . . two . . . one . . ."

"I would if I could," he said.

●

I was seventeen that summer. I had long brown hair prone to knots, thick eyebrows, an oversized nose, and duck lips. I weighed 110 pounds. I favored plaid bell-bottoms and Clark treks. I ate a head of iceberg lettuce for my lunch, in the manner of eating an apple. I had a little Smith Corona typewriter on which I pecked out letters to my congressman. During the school year I liked to annoy teachers I found lacking. One day in the spring I placed a snail on my French teacher's desk before he arrived at class, and the results exceeded my hopes. One look at it and he launched into a tirade about the person who had committed the deed, describing the perpetrator as "a dweller in the house of filth"—the most he'd ever said to us in any language, because he didn't speak French and most days sat frozen on a stool playing us tapes. As if holding the innocent mollusk personally to blame, he picked it up and hurled it at the wall, the shell shattering into many pieces and the moist, sluggish body tumbling to the floor. Then he grabbed his briefcase and stormed from the room, and I began to laugh so hysterically I cracked the corners of my mouth.

I was restless and bored and slightly unhinged by all the ups and downs at home. Missing the point, Mom and Roy thought I needed to get away from bad influences and enrolled me in a summer-school thing in northern California. Perfect. I had a boyfriend I wanted to spend time with, and now, miles from home, he'd come visit and I'd be able to. His name was Archer Upfield III.

Archie's parents were old. His father was an airline executive who'd gone mad. They lived in a big decaying house in the Encino hills. Never mind that the pool was green and filled with algae, the Scandinavian furniture bought expensively in the fifties now swarming with dust mites, the kitchen Formica cracked and cluttered with washed-out cottage cheese containers and lids, empty egg cartons stacked like one caterpillar mounting another, and newspapers in piles so long-standing you could smell the pulp breaking down. No, never mind. Archer felt privileged.

My house was down the street. Just a regular house but supposedly a step up from our last one. Mom had been having some medical problems the past year, and she and Roy had thought moving again would cheer her up. It hadn't.

"That tree is going to obliterate our view," Mom complained. It became something she was saying every day. "We finally move to a house with a view, and now it's going to be ruined."

The sapling across the street tickled the bottom of our view. It was a small tree, a sycamore, planted in the innocent hope that it would grow into a shapely specimen such as the ones that line the streets in European capitals, to be admired by the neighbors strolling past. It was not a bad tree. Except to my mother.

"What will we do?" she said. "That tree will soon block out everything we've worked for."

"It's just a smoggy valley. Can't you relax and be happy?"

"I'm trying, Ann. Wait until you're my age."

I met Archer when I moved to this neighborhood. We'd attended the same school all along but he'd never noticed me before. Now we sat at the back of the bus and kissed on the ride home. The bus driver yelled at us, things like, "Do I gotta hose you two down?" to which Archie would reply, "Keep thine eyes on the road, Civil Servant."

Then we'd say goodbye at the corner and, kicking rocks along the ground the rest of the way home, I'd brace myself for the latest batch of bad news.

It was the next-door neighbors. They rode motorcycles to and fro at all hours, tinkered with them in the yard, roasted boars in a pit, shot at beer cans with pop guns, and had been told to conceal these habits while we were buying the house. "If we call the police, they'll retaliate," Mom mused, one night at dinner.

"We'll move again if we have to," Roy said.

"We can't let them bully us," Mom said. "From now on, every time I drive by, I'm going to smile and wave."

"That will be terrifying," I said.

"Why?"

"You'll seem totally psychotic."

"I'm giving it a try," Mom said.

If I happened to be a passenger in the car when she smiled and waved, I saw what resulted. The son, a hulking twenty-year-old with greasy hair and legs like woolly cannons, narrowed his eyes in disbelief. I began to duck. "Stop!" I'd gasp.

"This might turn everything our way," Mom said, waving as we rolled down the street. Doubled over in the seat next to her, I'd say, "I don't think it's going to work."

After a spark plug flew over the fence and hit Kathy in the eyeball, Mom's next plan of attack involved sending me over with a plate of cookies.

"Hello," I muttered, when a woman in an orange muumuu answered the door. At least I thought it was a woman. She looked like a mechanic in a wig.

"Girl Scouts?" she said.

"My mother made these for you."

"Your mother?" she said. "Listen, nobody's doing any harm over here. You people act like we're dismembering babies. You gotta live and let live. Right?"

"Right," I said. "Want these cookies?"

"I'm trying to lose this gut, but what are they?"

"Chocolate chip."

"Margarine or butter?"

"Um, I think half and half."

"They got nuts in them?"

"Walnuts."

"Yeah, all right. Thanks. Tell your folks to take it easy."

She grabbed the plate from me, clamping her cigarette in her lips as she pushed open the screen door. I trudged home.

More than anything, I wanted to live in a world where people laughed and had fun. A world free for one day from strife. Lately, a world of menace and threat was the only world Mom knew. She either thought we were coming down with horrible diseases, or that neighbors and plants were encroaching on her territory, or that someone didn't like her, that we didn't have enough money, that my sister and I weren't sending enough letters to our one or two acceptable relatives, that the rosebushes were dying, that we were spilling grease on our clothing, that there would soon be a war in the Middle East, that we would be robbed or burglarized, or that her favorite crocks might break in a quake. There was never a moment when we could relax. As far as she was concerned, the more we were trembling with fear, the better.

When I returned from delivering the cookies, I said, "You know, they're not doing any harm over there. We act like they're disemboweling babies."

"Are you serious? This is our fault?"

"Well, maybe it is."

"It's our fault we can't sleep because they have parties at all hours? It's our fault their deadbeat son uses obscenities when speaking to me?"

"People should learn to live and let live," I said.

"Maybe you should just move next door!" my mother said. "Maybe you'd rather be part of their family!"

"All I'm saying is Mrs. Dogey seemed somewhat nice."

"She liked my cookies?" Mom said.

"Yeah, I think she did."

"Okay, wait and see. *Wait and see.*"

She'd say this whenever she was foisting something new on us. For example, because Kathy collected kangaroos, Mom had been convinced I should collect something. Detecting in me a slight attraction to owls, she pounced. Word got out. From then on I was receiving owl items whenever I was due for a gift.

Though I complained and raged, owls were halfway decent. Rather handsome, with their thumb-shaped bodies and big eyes, they had more presence than most birds. The way an octopus is better than a fish. But not instead of books and records and clothes. And who wanted to be pegged as an "owl person"? At night from my bed I gazed up at the shelf that displayed my enlarging collection and felt something bordering on despair. I wondered why children were encouraged to amass large quantities of animal bric-a-brac. Was it supposed to keep us engaged in life, through the quest to find more? Give us some phony sense of accomplishment as our collections grew? Keep our wants pure?

"You'll appreciate them someday," Mom said. "Wait and see."

"You know what?" I said. "Collecting stuff's a drag."

"Ann, there's nothing wrong with collecting things. Most girls do."

"I collect kangaroos," Kathy said.

"Oh, big wow, you're so cool," I said.

"How pleasant you are," Mom observed. "Wait until you go to college."

"Then what?"

"You'll miss us," she said.

Would I? When Mom finally escaped, her years at Vassar were *the time of her life*. I'd heard so much about it, it seemed like nothing else ever lived up to it, so much so it made me wonder if having *the time of your life* was even a good idea. She and her roommate would ride the train into New York; once, the night before such an outing, Mom dreamed a produce man was cursing and chasing them down the street. Next day, flitting around Greenwich Village, they knocked into a fruit stand and a produce man cursed and chased them down the street. They ducked into a subway, laughing and gasping for breath. She felt like her own person for the first time in her life. Not for long. What a thorn I must have been in her side. Imagine having a baby when you were still a kid, a colicky baby from what I've been told, a screamer all night long. No help from her parents, just harsh words and told-you-sos. A new job, finding all those babysitters, hard to keep track of it all.

Nana was my favorite. She had her own grandchildren, but we paid her to spend time with me and act like a grandmother. On Friday nights we'd drive her home and watch her amble up the walk with her bag, open the door, and disappear inside.

I wouldn't miss them. I knew how to resist feeling that.

The place they sent me that summer had sandstone-colored buildings and was as brown as a lion, all dry grass and windy oaks. My roommate, Hannah, was from Chico, the daughter of a surgeon, a party girl. She was bronzed by hours of poolside lounging, her perfect tan set off by the puka shells she wore at all times around her neck. She also had a plastic bag full of marijuana in her suitcase as big as a submarine sandwich. "Like to get stoned?" she asked me, our first day there.

"Never really have," I admitted.

"Oh, man, you're in for a treat. Let's roll up a doob right now."

"Yeah, sure," I said. "Might as well try it."

Listening to "Miracles" on Hannah's tape deck, I soon fell into a reverie about having sex with Archie. I tried to imagine all the things we'd never done—which included about everything. After a while I opened my eyes and saw Hannah organizing her string bikinis on her bed. It looked like she was spelling something with them. I changed into my suit, and off we went to sprawl beside the pool.

Letters soon poured in from Mom.

Please write and describe exactly what your room is like, what pieces of furniture are in it, and what you've put on the walls. What does Hannah look like? Do you eat together? Do you have nice conversations? What are her interests? How are your classes? Are you finding Art History as interesting as you thought you would? What text is your class using? Is your professor a real member of the faculty or just a summer-school teacher? Does he/she know your name? Is the food of good quality, and are the menus varied? Where do the other juniors come from? Do you think you and Hannah will remain friends? Are the bathroom facilities clean? Is there privacy? Do you keep your room locked at all times? Have there been any thefts?

I'd stare at the letter, then fold it up and put it into a drawer.

Three weeks along, Archie arrived in his hiccuping old Saab. I couldn't wait for him to see the new me. I was as tanned as Hannah by then, I'd learned how to knock down tequila in shots, and I'd been having fascinating discussions with a guy on my hall about how neither side of his brain was dominant, like Leonardo da Vinci's. But Archie took all the changes in stride. Within the first few minutes of his arrival, he had pulled out a map to show me the routes he planned to cycle during his visit.

"This one's an ass-buster," he said gleefully. "My brother did it once. Up into the hills, along the crest, down the other side to the ocean. Maybe you could come pick me up."

"But won't that take all day?"

"I'm not sure," he said. "I'll get an early start."

"God. I thought we were going to be hanging out together," I said.

"We are! Why do you think I came all the way up here?"

"Oh, good," I said. I kissed him.

That night in the dining hall I introduced him to my new friends. It made me feel important, having a visitor from the outside.

"Nice bike," Dwight, a guy from our hall, said. "Is that the same kind of Peugeot Nils Brennerhof used for the Tour de France?"

"Exactly," Archie said. "You into racing?"

"How much is that thing worth?"

"Got it used, fixed it up, and I could still sell it for nearly a grand."

"Thought so."

After dinner, Archie and I walked around the campus holding hands. His knuckles felt oversized. He was my first real boyfriend. He came all this way to see me.

"I ran into your mother last week at Gelson's," Archie said. "She turned around and went the other way."

"Maybe she didn't see you."

"She saw me, all right. She hates my guts. Don't worry, I think it's funny. I wouldn't *want* her to like me."

"Why not?"

"Because then it would mean I was some kind of eunuch, probably."

"My mother doesn't like eunuchs."

"I betcha she does," Archie said.

It wasn't the time to argue. We ended up back in my room, and I locked the door and turned out the lights. I was proud of the smell of the magnolia flowers drifting in through the windows, and proud to have all this freedom to offer, more valuable to me than gold coins in a purse. I led him to my bed.

"Come here," I said.

Archie liked exploring my ears with his tongue. But when I tried to play with his belt, he giggled like I was tickling him.

"Whoa," he said.

"Okay."

"I'll do it," he said. But he didn't.

"You know what I think is weird?" I said.

"What."

"You know how, in movies, they often show wives not wanting to have sex, like pretending they have a headache or something?"

"Yeah."

"Well, I don't understand it. If I were married, I'd never feel that way."

"Oh. Really."

We continued to kiss, but now he seemed on guard. He strayed from my lips and kissed my ears and suddenly the flickering of his tongue became a rope coiling into my head.

"Wait," I said. "No!"

Twisting, coiling—his mouth swallowed my ear. The inner ear exploded. Something warm was running down my neck, onto my shoulder. I staggered up and groped for the switch. In the bright dorm-room light we found ourselves clotted with blood.

"Jesus!" Archie screamed.

"Oh, my God."

"Oh, gross, do something!"

"What should I do?"

"Get a towel!" he said.

"Could you please get the towel?"

"Gross!" he yelled. "Gross!"

He was jumping and wiping himself off, clawing at his clothes. I found a washcloth and held it to my head.

"Why did you do that?" I said miserably.

"It's supposed to feel good," he said.

"I can barely hear out of it."

"Get it to stop bleeding!"

As we headed for the showers, hustling out of my room, Archie pulled the door closed behind us. It locked.

"Oh, no!"

"Hey, cut the moaning." He reared up on one leg and kicked. The door frame ripped and cracked and splintered. He kicked at it again and again. Finally the door fanned open, and a chunk of wood dangled and dropped to the floor.

"Oh, God, why did you do that?"

"Stupid door," Archie said.

"What's so stupid about it?"

"Screw this, I'm taking a shower," Archie said.

Through the night my ear throbbed as if mounted on my head with a nail. The messed-up door rattled and banged. First thing in the morning I visited the campus doctor. She took one look and referred me to an off-campus specialist, and I was able to get an appointment immediately. My balance was a little off but I rode my bike in slow motion. The specialist cleared out some of the dried blood and peered at my eardrum and promptly told me it had been perforated. In addition to the perforation there was a large area where the tissue had been pulled apart, like layers of baklava. "How in the world did this happen?" he asked.

"It's kind of unpleasant, but—well, my boyfriend was kissing my ear," I said, "and then I guess he created some kind of giant plunger with his mouth."

"Time to get a new boyfriend," the doctor said.

He said it might take a few months to heal, maybe longer. He said to keep it dry in the shower and when swimming. He said the chances of permanent hearing loss were slim, but I might have ringing or crackling in my ears for some time to come. He whisked out more of the dried blood with a tiny vacuum. It hurt.

The bill was $127. I didn't have it. I had only $56, to be used for miscellaneous necessities. All afternoon while Archie was out on his bike, I fretted.

"You'll help me out with it, won't you?" I asked Archie that evening.

"It's a farce," he said. "They'll never make you pay."

"What about part of it?"

"I don't have it right now. I'm working full time and I owe my brother a thousand bucks for the car."

"It doesn't seem fair I have to pay it all."

"That's what I'm telling you," he said. "Don't."

Meanwhile, a large man in overalls came to fix the door frame. No small job. It involved several hours of fitting and drilling. A few days after Archie left, I found an envelope under the door. It contained a bill for $210, saying that failure to remit would result in the withholding of any transcript generated by my current undertaking.

I could be resourceful. This past winter, Mom was in and out of the hospital for tests. Something was wrong with her endocrine system. She started reading medical journals, coming to her appointments ready with the answers. "I'm convinced that the paresthesias and tetany I've experienced recently are a result of primary aldosteronism. My hypertension is resistant to medication. I'm highly edematous, and the levels of K in my urine are always high. I'd recommend a CT scan to detect the presence of adenomas in the adrenals and, if negative, pursue secondary aldosteronism as a sequela to renal vasoconstriction. Are we on the same page?" Doctors weren't wild about her approach, and she was gloomy.

"Is it possible," I'd said, "that you're playing out your relationship to your absent mother with these doctors? Fighting with them or else showing off your medical knowledge as a roundabout way of capturing her approval?"

"I don't want my mother's approval!" she'd said, indignantly.

"Everyone wants their mother's approval," I'd said, accidentally.

To cheer her up, I had gone with my friend Roberta to find Bob Dylan's new house in Malibu. I wanted to get Mom an autograph. She enjoyed the early stuff, especially when other people performed it. The house had been written up in the *LA Times*—a huge sprawling monster made up of different architectural styles. It even had a Russian onion dome on one side.

In Malibu it was easy to find, bathed in floodlights and

surrounded by a chain-link fence. The grounds still had the rough appearance of a construction site. "Hard to believe no one else is here," I said, as we parked on the quiet street.

"Yeah," Roberta said. "I kind of expected a thronging crowd."

"Me too."

The gate was closed, the fence too shaky to climb. We clawed at the dirt instead. After a while, we pulled the links away from the ground and wiggled under like gophers. Inside, we brushed the dirt from our knees. We had soil jammed under our fingernails and rinsed our hands with a shiny brass nozzle on a garden hose. We combed our hair and put gloss on our lips. Then we sauntered up to the front door. Two guys were hammering and sawing just inside the entryway, one tall and blond, the other blond and tall, and when they spotted us, their tools stalled.

"What are you girls doing here?" said one.

"Um, we were driving by and saw you guys working, and thought it looked intriguing," said Roberta.

"Yes, this is a very intriguing job," the other said.

"It's Bob Dylan's house, isn't it?" I said.

"No, it's Mick Jagger's," the first said, very sarcastically.

"Right!" we laughed.

They introduced themselves as Edric and Fane, brothers from Jutland.

"Want a look around?" Edric said.

They gave us a tour through the whole place. The house was huge and ungainly. I wondered why Bob Dylan had chosen to spend his money this way. They showed us all the custom-made cabinets and fixtures and it bugged me to imagine Bob picking them out. There was an enormous bathroom with a tub the size of a pool, decorated with tile they said came from a pharaoh's tomb. The grout glittered with real gold.

"So what's he like?" Roberta asked, after they'd surrounded us in a swirling cloud of smoke.

"We're not supposed to talk." Fane coughed.

"Strict orders." Edric inhaled.

"Oh, come on, just tell us one thing," she said.

Edric said, "What can we tell them?"

Fane said, "Hmm. What about the cucumbers?"

"Yes, that's right, he really *loves* cucumbers," Edric giggled. "Come look."

They led us back into a little chamber off the restaurant-sized kitchen. "This room will be solely dedicated to his cucumbers," Edric said.

"It's the cucumber room," Fane said.

"You guys are comic geniuses," Roberta said.

They both began to cackle. Fane grabbed Roberta and tried to kiss her. She screamed.

"We showed you the house," he said. "Come on!"

"Can't you meet girls any other way?" Roberta demanded.

"We don't need to meet girls," Edric said.

"They need to meet us," Fane said.

"Look, I brought this," I said quickly. It was *Tarantula*, a book of Dylan's poetry and ideas, stuffed in an envelope addressed to my mother. "My Mom's a big fan, in fact it's one of the main things we have in common, and she's been a little sick lately. I was wondering if he could sign this and send it to her."

Fane shrugged. "What do we get in return?"

"All he has to do is put it in the mail."

"You thought of everything," Edric said.

"Almost everything," Fane said, moving toward me.

"Let's go," Roberta said.

"Thanks, I really mean it," I said, and we went running out the front door.

We drove back to the valley, laughing hard. At one point I said, "You think they'll do it, even though we didn't make out with them?"

"I'd say there's about as much chance as me inviting Dan Rather to the prom, and him saying yes."

We thought dark-haired Dan was a dynamo. "By the way, I still think you should."

"Okay. And you can invite Walter Cronkite."

"Ha-ha!" We snorted and laughed.

Even so, from then on, I would come home from school hoping Mom had gotten the package in the mail. Stranger things had happened. You never knew.

●

I now owed $337.

"Just get it over with. Ask your parents," Hannah said. Her parents paid for her to get her toenails done.

"My mother wouldn't like it," I said.

"Well, maybe Archie'll change his mind and chip in," she said.

I didn't want to be seen as surrounded by tightwads. "Right. I'm going to call him, somehow, tonight."

That afternoon I found myself scanning the bulletin board in the employment office. A notice for yard work caught my eye and, from a phone booth outside, I called. The job wasn't taken! After I described my yard-work experiences, the woman gave me directions and invited me right over.

My tires hummed on the hot concrete, while the air smelled of palm resin and drying grass. There were old oaks and redwoods scattered around these neighborhoods, wild creek beds to cross, and real squirrels running along the phone lines. I found myself rolling up to a little gingerbread-type house, with copper butterflies mounted on the lintel and with a personalized mat welcoming me.

The Holcombs. An older woman appeared at the door, the pleasant kind that probably played bridge or went to church or made large happy Thanksgiving dinners for her children and grandchildren without outbursts or fuss. She took me into her world, past her cozy plaid couch and cabinet full of animal figurines, out again through a sliding glass door. There she showed me a big mound thriving with birds-of-paradise.

"You pull this part back and this thing pops out and then you take off the old dried leaves back here and now the face can shine out. See?"

With her knobby fingers she managed to preen one. It involved opening the blossom on the bird-of-paradise to its fullest potential. They tended to get trapped in their own armature.

"Good," she said, when I completed one. "My hands are frozen stiff with arthritis; otherwise I'd do it myself."

I kind of enjoyed it too. "That's all you want me to do?"

"Let's see how it goes. I've got a boy who comes and does the grass."

"So I guess you really like birds-of-paradise," I said.

"They're very special," she said.

"Do you worry about them?" I asked. "Like, if they're all going to die, or get diseased, or not enough water, stuff like that?"

"Well I'd rather spend my time enjoying them. Now if you see any snails, peel them off."

She had just found one, and she threw it on the grass and stomped on it.

We agreed that I'd come by twice a week to start. What a stroke of good luck! She also provided sandwiches and root beer, and I didn't even know that yet.

Someone was pounding on our door.

Hannah opened up to the ox from Orinda. "This is a first," she said.

"What are these calls to Encino doing on my phone bill?"

I stepped forward.

"It was you on my line, wasn't it. I thought it was. You owe me seventeen dollars and twenty-five cents."

More money. I found my checkbook.

"Were you tapping my line because of my family's connection to the Nixons?"

"Yeah, I was hoping I could hear you and your parents

talking about being friends with the Nixons, because I haven't heard enough about it yet, even though you've told everybody probably five times."

"We don't talk about it on the phone," she said.

"Hey, could I make another call right now, and write you another check?"

"This is the way it's done. I'm going to time you."

I followed her down the hall to her room, which was a single because she'd paid extra not to have to *share*.

"Whose phone are you on this time?" Archie said, not even sounding too excited it was me.

"Listen," I said, "go to my house and tell my mother there's a garden nozzle you need and it's on the shelf with my owls."

"Why?"

"It's really valuable. I'm not sure I'll make enough at my job, and maybe I can sell it."

"A nozzle?"

"Guess whose it is."

"Whose?"

"Bob Dylan's!"

"What are you doing with Bob Dylan's nozzle?" he said.

The Orinda girl was staring at her watch. "I'll tell you some other time."

"Wait a minute, who's going to believe you?"

"Why wouldn't they?" I said.

"Is there any *proof* it's Bob Dylan's nozzle?"

"Of course it's his nozzle, why would I make it up?"

"What, is it, like, *engraved* or something?"

"Of course not, why would you even say that?"

"It's a pretty lame idea," he said.

"Two minutes," the Orinda girl said.

"Forget it then," I said. "I didn't want to sell it anyway."

"Was that really your big idea?" He laughed.

"My big idea is that I'm going to enjoy hanging up right now," I said, and I did enjoy it, though I had to write another check.

That summer, the least of it was my classes. The bird-of-paradise woman increased my hours, and I was spending whole afternoons with her. I fed the birds-of-paradise with fish emulsion and kept all weeds at bay. I learned how to separate overcrowded clumps and start new colonies in various corners of the yard. I maintained beds of annuals and pruned a vibrant eugenia hedge. I rescued plums from the birds and wove tendrils of jasmine onto a bald fence. My ear clicked and crackled the faster I worked, but all the industry made the bird-of-paradise woman look out her back door and smile.

While I ate my tuna sandwich full of pickles, she often mentioned her dead husband, Conrad. "Conrad used to hate weekends," she'd say. "He detested this town, he was so tired of all the students and coffee shops." "Conrad used to sit there all weekend; I couldn't get him to budge." And Conrad had complained about her cooking. "It was never as good as his mother's, but that man could really wolf down a meal."

I was tempted to ask what she'd seen in Conrad, but no

matter what she told me, she spoke of him without rancor. I came from a family of anger and impulse. I couldn't imagine myself living for years with someone like Conrad. Or could I?

It stayed hot those days on the peninsula, the kind of scorching weather that kept the grass brown until the rains fell again in winter. I had a vision that kept me happy, of living in a creaky Victorian in San Francisco someday with a bunch of my friends. I'd have my own phone, and an orange cat sitting in a wicker chair in the sun. We'd all have odd jobs and come home at night with stories to tell.

Then, the last day of summer school, after paying off the college bursar and the ear specialist, I rode my bike over to say goodbye to the bird-of-paradise woman. She had prepared a plump sack of oatmeal cookies for my journey, and I threw my arms around her, wishing for a moment she was my own grandmother, or at least someone I didn't have to say goodbye to. I had the impulse to love somebody too quickly and desperately, I could see that much. I'd have to be careful of that.

There were parties, address exchanges. "What're you going to do about Archie?" Hannah asked.

"Not much. I have a lot of studying to do this year," I said.

"I wish we got to know each other better. Let's for sure stay in touch, okay?"

"For sure!"

She gave me a Smith College T-shirt that said A CENTURY OF WOMEN ON TOP. She'd gained early admittance, knew her life's course. Party girl that she was, she wanted to go into the diplomatic corps and later did just that. But for now we all packed and vacated the dorm one Saturday morning before noon, just kids going home, and Hannah's young, attractive parents gave me and my bike a lift to the bus station. They made jokes about how in the world had I put up with a scoundrel like Hannah, I must be a saint, and so forth, but they were beaming at their daughter and their daughter was beaming at them. It was a love fest. I couldn't wait to get out of the car.

Roy picked me up twelve hours later. I was stuffed with oatmeal cookies, dirty and tired and sore. "Welcome home," he said, jamming my things into the back. "How'd it all go?"

I had to turn my head and point my good ear at him. "Not bad," I said. "How's everything at home?"

"Not too good," he said. "We'll probably start looking to move."

"Again?"

"No use hassling over it all. We're not attached to the place anyway. Are you?"

"It's my senior year," I said. "I don't want to change schools."

"We'll try to keep you at the same school," he said. "Don't worry about that."

"How's Mom?"

"Your mother is a great human being."

"I mean, is she feeling okay?"

"She has a lot on her plate. No more trouble; do we have an understanding?"

"I just got home!"

"Well, do we?"

"Yes! God!"

Soon we pulled up in the driveway of our now designated non-home. The sight of it made me sick, like being greeted by a crippled old dog you've decided to take out behind the barn. Mom and Kathy rushed out to meet me. There were hugs and hellos all around.

"Did you have the time of your life?" Mom asked.

"I hope not."

"Why, what's wrong?"

"Did you bring me anything?" Kathy said.

I did have something for Kathy, and I groped numbly for it in my bag.

"What is it?" she asked when I handed it to her.

"A gerenuk."

"What's a gerenuk?"

"It's an animal from Africa. I thought maybe you could start a collection."

She frowned at the gerenuk. "One's probably enough."

Mom said, "Behold," and pointed to the sycamore, which had grown in my absence to further obscure the view.

"Oh, well," I said.

"Oh, well, is right," she said. "We're moving before anything else goes wrong!"

We all gathered around the kitchen table, and it was nice because they wanted to hear about my adventures, though I deleted the ear thing and substituted "a guy on my hall" for Archie in the story of my door. Mom seemed shocked by some of the things she hadn't known. "You had a *job*?" she said. "You went to this woman's home off campus? What kind of person was this? You ate there?" After she calmed down, since, after all, I'd only just arrived, she said, "Well, she sounds like a very nice woman. You'll have to send her a thank-you card immediately." And since I'd only just arrived, I couldn't say, "Back off!" could I? But I made them laugh, describing the girl from Orinda and her Nixon-mania, among other tales of dorm life. It was fun making them laugh.

That evening, unpacking in my room, eager to call my friends and announce my return, wondering what I'd be facing next, I found myself gazing idly for a moment at my shelf of owls. Something was missing: my beautiful nozzle! I ran to the den and asked Mom if she'd seen it.

"The nozzle on your shelf? I needed it."

I ran outside. We had a bunch of hoses in our yard, stationed in various places. A thick aqua-colored one, a thin-skinned dark green one, a short stiff one, a crackled one, one with a stripe. In the moonlight, I could see each had a nozzle attached. While the hoses were different, the nozzles looked identical.

"Which hose did you use it on?" I cried, running back in.

"I don't remember," my mother said. "Why does it matter?"

"You've got to. Was it the one by the door?"

"Maybe. I honestly can't say."

"Was it the one out by the fence, where the tomatoes are?"

"Ann, calm down."

"Come on, think!"

Mom said, "I don't remember, and you're making me extremely tense."

I started to cry. My life was a ruin. There was no hope for me anytime, anywhere.

"What's going on, was it a special nozzle?" she said.

"Yes."

"Did Archie give it to you?" she asked, smoothing my hair.

"No!" I said. "I hate Archie," I added.

"I'm not surprised," Mom said. "He was arrogant and narcissistic, and I couldn't stand him, frankly."

"God, couldn't you have asked me, about the nozzle?"

My mother said, "You should have hidden it away, if it was so important."

"Oh, great, is that the way to live life?"

"Please go get some rest," she said.

I tossed. I turned. I was full of horrible feelings, feelings I couldn't name. I wanted to attack something. I *had* to attack something. I decided to attack the tree across the street.

I crept out of bed, slipped on a T-shirt and jeans, let myself out the back door. I moved stealthily down the driveway and across the street to inspect the small tree that truly was starting to block the so-called view. Up close, I could see it was larger than I'd thought. The trunk was a few inches thick at the base, and when I tried wiggling it, it barely budged.

No matter. I pushed it, kicked it, twisted it, threw myself at it. I ripped off its lower branches and bent it to the ground. I jumped on it, cracked it, split it. In so doing, I began to expose some of the roots.

I sawed and pounded and hacked at them with a stone. I tore at them. I lacerated whatever part of any root I could see. After nearly an hour, I was finally able to wrest the tree from the ground. At about twelve feet long, it was heavy.

I ran down the street, pulling the carcass along. It scraped the asphalt, leaves ripped and scattered, twigs jumped and snapped. At last I stood at the top of a small ravine, a dark area between two houses. I threw the murdered sapling like a javelin, and gravity brought it to rest with a shivering thud.

Then I walked home. My work was done. The night was warm, as it was late August in the valley. I lifted my T-shirt and let the air touch my skin, blotted my face with the hem of it. Then I found a place on the curb in front of our house and sat a moment, letting my heart slow down. My hands were grazed and torn but I hardly cared. I was still young and silly enough to wonder if what I'd just done might make a difference. Keep us from having to move again. Change the course of history. I couldn't wait for morning, when Mom would look out and realize her view was no longer being obstructed. At first I imagined her excitement about it, then wondered how long it would take her to find something else to worry about. I planned on keeping a perfectly straight face.

Look Out, Kids

It was a full-time job, cooking pizza and selling slices in a cinder-block bungalow on the beach in Santa Monica. All day from the counter I watched people frolicking and laughing and lying around with Frisbees and books and slices of our pizza on the warm white sand. Our pizza was good and we often had lines. In the back room I dragged bags of flour to the dough machine every couple of hours, mixed in the yeast and the oil and the water, and waited for it to rise into a big white lump like a naked stomach that hadn't been out on the beach all summer. Like, for example, my own.

I earned $2 an hour, so I made $80 a week. I was saving for college. No money to waste on clothes or records or concert tickets. I'd be up at seven, swigging down a cup of instant Maxim, out the door by seven-thirty in my family's old Buick station wagon with the cracking vinyl seats, down Sepulveda to Pico all the way to the beach to report by eight.

We had a new house, over the hill. My parents were the kind that didn't believe in giving anyone a free ride. My mother supposedly knew a Rockefeller while she was in college and was always impressed that he worked in a gas station on the side. That he was being taught the right values. There was no arguing that one. If a Rockefeller had to work his way through school, so did I.

Anyway, a lot of people had to work. I was no different.

It wasn't bad. For one thing, my first day on the job I met Jake. He had hair to his back pockets, longer and shinier than mine, and he played the harmonica during his ten-minute break out on the back stoop next to the Dumpster. That day he told me he'd just taken the Green Turtle to New York and back, sleeping on the floor of the gutted bus with the coolest people I could imagine, almost as cool as the Merry Pranksters.

I liked him.

One day, a week into the job, as I was about to put some proceeds into the cash register, Jake said, "Pause a moment. Are you actually satisfied with the slave wages we're getting here?"

I shrugged. "I guess. It's the going rate."

"The going rate for what?" he said. "Selling your youth?"

I laughed. "Don't think about it so much. A job's a job, right?"

"Yeah, but who keeps this place going, Sal or us?" Sal was the owner, a short, ugly small-time businessman who fancied himself with it by virtue of a few gold chains around his turkey-gobbler neck.

"I guess he pays for the ingredients," I replied.

"Okay, so he buys industrial-sized sacks of flour, wheels of the blandest cheese, and army-issue cans of sauce, and everything together probably costs him pennies. We carefully prepare it and stand here all day in a broiling shack."

All we had to do, according to Jake, was sell a couple of pieces of pizza every hour that we didn't ring up. Sixty cents each. After all, we were allowed to *eat* as much as we wanted to. It would only be the same as eating a couple more slices an hour, but we'd take the $1.20 or $1.80 in cash. Kind of like a tip. "I don't know," I said. "If you want to do it, go ahead. I won't tell anyone."

"I can't do it if you won't." He sulked.

"Suit yourself."

"What if you were a fatso? You'd be scarfing all day at Sal's expense," he said. "Which you're not, by the way. Fat. At all."

"If you think it's so bad here, why did you take the job?"

"How long did you look in the want ads?" Jake said. "It was this or a car wash in Venice or a stockroom in a light fixture store in Culver City."

I hadn't tried anywhere else.

Whenever I came home from work, my family would be waiting to see how much pizza I brought home (the day's leftovers, destined for the garbage). But it's not like we were poor. It's not like we couldn't buy our own pizza. Soon our freezer was full of pizza slices. We had enough to last for months. "This is quite a deal you have going," Roy said, chomping on his latest warmed-up slice. "We're going to miss it when it's over."

"It's just a bunch of dough," I said. "What's the big deal?"

"Good dough," Roy said.

Los Angeles is usually hot in the summer, but not where I was working. In the morning, fog covered the beach, and the cement building was chilly from absorbing the night air. Once the ovens were fired, we'd warm up, though. The sea breezes kept the place aired out.

One day Sal came in and reminded us that he'd need volunteers on the Fourth of July to keep the place open until midnight. We'd get double time. We'd get to see the fireworks out over the pier. Jake said no, but I needed the money and said I'd take the shift; then Jake changed his mind and said he would too.

"Might get rowdy down here," Sal told us. "Last year somebody tried to blow the place up. You sure you two can handle it?"

"We'll just hand out pizza and calm everybody down," Jake said.

"You better not," Sal said. "You want me to start keeping inventory? Too much work for all of us. But no funny stuff. You're using too much cheese," he said, biting into a square of what I'd made that morning in the fog. "Use the measuring cup. Don't get fancy."

"Okay," I said.

"What the hell is this?" Sal said, leaning over behind the tanks that made the fizz in the soft drinks. He picked up the book Jake brought in that morning, *Naked Lunch.* "Nobody's having any naked lunch on my time," he said, pocketing it.

●

The afternoons were long, especially when it was cloudy. The water turned the color of old broccoli, dog walkers clipped by in their sweats, and the only people coming up to our window were the local drunks that Jake had been extending Sal's charity to. It was the day he told me he was starting at Otis College of Art and Design in the fall, and asked what school I'd be attending. I said, "I'm not sure. I got into UC Santa Cruz, but I didn't get any financial aid, so I'm not sure I can go until I save up."

"Hey, no kidding, that's where my brother goes," Jake said. "Major hippie school."

"It's modeled on the Oxford system, and it's supposed to be excellent academically," I said.

"Yeah, everyone I've ever met up there was a space case. In a good way. Really cool folks. Artsy. That kind of place. Won't your parents help you out?"

"They would if they could."

"But how are you going to save anything working here?"

"It adds up," I said.

"That's insane. You're totally the college type." Per Sal's instructions, he was counting pepperoni like it was currency coming out of the cash drawer: twenty a pie, one every two inches. "You know," he said, "next weekend I'm driving up there to visit my brother. He's in summer school.

Why don't you come? It'll be hip, plus maybe you can talk to the financial aid people, change their minds."

"Change their minds?" The idea confused me. Was Financial Aid a real place I could actually go? They'd already turned me down based on my family's middle-class income, so how could I change their minds?

"Just go in there and see what they say," he insisted.

That night I told Mom and Roy what I wanted to do. Mom said, "Who is this boy? What kind of car does he have?"

I said, "It's an Opel Cadet. He's really nice. His dad's a chemistry professor at UCLA."

"I take it he likes you."

"No, he's just a friend," I said. "I guess we'll stay in his brother's dorm."

"Well, we have plenty of pizza in the freezer," Roy said. "We'll survive."

My mother said, "I don't know what you'll tell the financial aid people they don't already know. They eviscerated us. They know more about us than the IRS."

"I don't know," I said. "Maybe I can talk them into giving me a work-study grant."

"Give it the old college try," Roy said.

The details escape me now, but somehow I was able to call up and make an appointment. This, in itself, amazed me. Then Jake and I planned the trip all week, plotting how we would both call in sick at dawn on Friday and basically close the place down, unless Sal manned the counter by himself. The thought of him frantically baking and taking change at the order window cracked us up. And he wouldn't be able to fire us, since he'd be counting on us for Saturday night, the Fourth.

When Jake picked me up early Friday morning, the back of his car was full of clothes and books and records that his brother wanted from home, plus two sleeping bags that looked like they were already zipped together. Shoving my stuff in back, I saw a packet of condoms poking out of Jake's backpack. He pressed an eight-track tape into his deck and we started our journey listening to *Workingman's Dead,* which I'd never heard before.

●

Driving up 101 with Jake, I watched as he did a mysterious thing with his hands. He was holding them out, one at a time, and slowly manipulating his fingers, as if admiring at arm's length how they worked. He did it in slow motion. He always held his flexing hand in front of the air vent, and that's when I finally realized he was merely drying out his sweaty palms.

Just outside of Santa Barbara, Jake said, "I finally feel like I'm waking up."

"Me too," I said.

"I couldn't sleep last night. I was weirdly excited about this trip," he said.

"I bet you miss your brother," I mused.

"Yeah," he said. "But it wasn't that." He put on another tape, *Sweet Baby James.* At the time I thought James Taylor was boring and insipid, but since everybody else in the world loved him, I didn't say anything. "So," he said then, "are you, like, seeing anyone these days?"

"No," I said.

"I'm surprised, because you seem like the type who'd always have a boyfriend on hand somewhere."

"Nope," I said. "Not me." To make conversation, I said, "Are you?"

"Had a big breakup in the spring. Two years we were together. She left me for another guy. A total geek."

"Sorry," I said.

He smiled. "Are you hungry?"

"No."

"I brought some sandwiches. My mother made them. They're ham. Do you like ham?"

"When I'm hungry I like it," I said.

"Want to stop and take a walk on the beach, or should we just keep driving?"

"Maybe we should just keep driving," I said.

Jake nodded. He changed the subject. He said he had a big surprise for his brother, patting his pocket, as if I'd know what that meant. I didn't.

At that point in my life, I guess I was what you would call square. I did what I had to do, more or less; I didn't stay out late at night; I studied; I went to bed. That kind of kid. I wasn't exactly happy, but my life philosophy wasn't very well developed. I expected things to get better. Without realizing it at the time, I subscribed heartily to *delayed gratification*.

For example, whenever someone gave me a usable item, like a candle or a bar of soap, I'd never use it. I'd save it for later. Years would go by. Seriously, I had dust-caked candles I'd won at parties in fourth grade. I had bars of soap from my great-aunt that were cracked with age. I was eighteen years old. What was I waiting for?

My appointment at the Financial Aid office was at three, and we rolled into Santa Cruz right on time. Up we went through the town to the university, which was located on an old ranch of open fields and redwood forests on some gentle hills overlooking the sea.

"Tell those cheapskates the regents are overpaid and to give you some cash," Jake said, letting me out in front of the curiously ugly cement structure.

"Thanks," I said. "Where should I meet you?"

"I'll come back and pick you up, how about."

"No, go see your brother," I said. "I'll find you."

"Yeah, okay," he said. "Winston's at College Five. So just walk through the woods thataway and I'll look for you in about an hour in the coffeehouse. Don't get lost, okay?"

"Okay," I said.

"We're going to have fun tonight," he called out after me.

I waved.

"See you!" he called.

I waved again.

Then I stepped into the building and found the office

where they would decide my fate. A man with curly black hair wearing a Hawaiian shirt greeted me. His name was Arnie Buckman.

"Hello, Ann," he said. "Come sit down. Can I offer you some tea?"

Already things seemed promising. He made me some spicy tea, then took a seat at his desk. He had a folder with my name on it and he flipped it open and gave me a rundown on how they'd done their figuring and why I'd been denied. Now he said he'd be happy to reconsider if I had any further information.

"I do," I said.

And so I began.

"Maybe on paper it doesn't look so bad," I said, "but you see, in the past year, we—my family—had a run of bad luck. It all started when an idiotic, uptight professional clown with dancing poodles, seventeen of them if you can believe it, moved in next door to us. We weren't overreacting. Anyone would have been unhappy about it. This was the house we expected to stay in for some time to come. Things had been stable before this happened. My stepfather went to work, came home, we all had dinner, that kind of family. My mother had some problems, sure, but the system worked. We all pitched in to make it all right. So along came this horrible clown man, and his poodles barked all day long, and my mother is very sensitive and she started to deteriorate. It's not like she's an alcoholic or anything. But she's rather reclusive and our house is like her sanctuary. So we had no choice but to move."

He nodded and took notes, so I continued.

"We found a house nearby that seemed perfect at first, although it needed a number of expensive repairs before we moved in. Then, within a month, we discovered that the teenage son next door was part of a motorcycle gang. The gang was always roaring up to the house on their motorcycles, and then they'd party loudly with the radio blasting. I guess they got angry about the complaints because they started throwing things over the fence, including a greasy alternator that went through my parents' bedroom window. It was the last straw. My mother was practically catatonic. We realized we had no choice but to move again."

"That must have been very upsetting," Arnie Buckman said.

"Yes, it was. My mother's health problems were really flaring up. Some of them nobody could figure out. The doctors treated her horribly, as if she were some kind of hypochondriac. So to relieve her from the stress that might cut short her existence, they decided to put all our stuff into storage, take all our savings and go away for a while. We spent some time in Australia. For weeks we rode around the country on trains, north to south, east to west. Standard gauge and narrow gauge, whatever it took. I think we saw everything you could see from a train in that country. I personally could have done without the second trip across the Nullarbor Plain, which consists of two thousand miles of absolute nothingness, but the spare conditions seemed just the ticket for my mother. She cheered up. When we ran out of money we came back and had to stay in a motel for about three months, and just a few months ago, halfway through my senior year, they finally found another house—not that great but more expensive because real estate's gone up—and that's when they broke the news to me they'd spent my college savings on the trip, and they were completely broke."

"Yikes," Arnie Buckman said.

"I wasn't sure you could tell all that from the application."

"No," he said. "We couldn't. On the form all we see are the numbers. How are your parents doing now?"

"Okay," I said. "The people next door to us on both sides are old and quiet, so my mother is relaxing."

"And your stepfather's job?"

"He likes to say that if he'd stayed in the private sector, he'd be making a killing, but since he made a career change into education—well, it's just not as remunerative."

"But it's secure?"

"Oh, yes," I said. "They gave him time off when my mother was sick, and now he has to stay there for years."

"And you?"

"I'm working full time and should have about eight hundred dollars saved by September."

"Very good," he said. "Well. It was a pleasure to meet you. We'll see what we can do."

I smiled. "Wow. Thanks!"

"And Ann," he called after me, "try and have a little fun this summer too, okay?"

"Fun? Okay!"

I'd never exposed all that stuff to anyone before, and I felt strangely revitalized. I kicked up duff all the way through the redwoods to College Five and found a table in the coffeehouse. I was starving. Because Mom and Roy never took us out to eat, even ordering a sandwich in a student coffeehouse was exciting for me. I ordered turkey and avocado on whole wheat, but forgot to say hold the sprouts. I pulled the green whiskers out of the sandwich before I ate it, and it was still good. It had an immense dill pickle with it, and some olives.

Since Jake and his brother weren't there, I decided to take off and tour all the colleges of the campus. This way I could decide which one I liked best. As it turned out, the colleges were quite spread out, and one could walk for a long time surrounded only by redwood trees without seeing a building or a person. It took me longer than I expected to reach each one. I stopped and had an ice cream cone at another coffeehouse. Then I wandered down a footpath to the sports center and checked out the facilities. I hiked over to the Performing Arts center. All good. Last but not least, I inspected the library. It had a great spiral staircase and everything was clearly marked and easy to find. I ended up in the basement investigating the periodical section and settling into a comfortable chair with a few journals ripe with articles such as "Quantifier Scope and Syntactic Islands" and "On the Nontransformational Derivation of Some Null NP Anaphors." Great stuff, clearly.

Later, when I found my way back to College Five, I wasn't too surprised Jake wasn't there waiting for me. I was pretty late. In fact, it was almost dark. The coffeehouse was about to close when I saw the two of them stumbling across the quad in my direction.

"What happened?" Jake cried. "We waited forever!" His cheeks were red, his pupils big as marbles.

"Oh, I was looking around."

"I was worried! God! Everything got totally messed up. I wish you would've left a note or something," he said. "By the way, this is Winston."

Jake's brother bowed. He didn't look like Jake at all. He was chubby and wore suspenders, and his hair was frizzy as a tumbleweed. "To many I'm known as the Hode," he said.

"Did you get money?" Jake asked.

"I don't know yet."

"We ate some psilocybin," he said. "Sorry."

"They feel so long and spindly," Winston said, looking at his hands.

"I was thinking you might want to try some," Jake said. "Want to try some?"

"No, thanks," I said.

"Mind-altering," he said. "Keeps getting more intense, like your brain's a mouth opening wider and wider. I wish you could be here, you know, it's like love and everything in the universe is right here. Within reach. It's just right here around me, like a cape. Right, brother?"

"Right," Winston said.

In Winston's room, which was festooned with tapestries and fabrics, had stereo speakers the size of refrigerators, and was quickly empty of Winston, I saw that Jake's double sleeping bag had already been laid out. I saw that my bag had been brought in for me, and that Jake's bag was next to it. I saw that two pillows had been placed at the top of the double sleeping bag for our heads. But Jake seemed restless and uncomfortable. He was pacing and wringing his hands. "It seems stuffy in here, don't you think? Wouldn't you rather sleep outside?"

"You can, if you want," I said.

"I'm not sure I can get in that bag right now," he said. "I think I need some air."

"That's okay," I said.

"You ever tried this stuff?" he said.

"No," I said.

"Man, it's really amazing, it's like everything is so rich. You are beautiful, did you know I thought so?"

"Thanks," I said.

"Winston says you're beautiful, and he knows."

"Oh. Well, thanks."

"You could rule the world," he said.

"I doubt it," I said.

"I think I need to go outside," he said. "I feel kind of sick."

"I can tell," I said.

"I'll just take a little walk," he said.

"Good idea," I said.

"I'll see you in a little while, and I'm really looking forward to that."

"Me too," I said.

He went out the door, closed it, then promptly came back in. "That felt good," he said. He leaned up against the wall and slid down it until he was curled in a ball at the baseboard. "So, you like to dance?"

"Sure."

"But not disco, right?"

"No, I hate disco."

"The Bee Gees, they're stupid, don't you think?"

"Horrible," I said.

"You know, I wasn't going to mention this, but Sal thinks we're an item. Thinks we've been messing around in the storage room."

"He does?"

"Like it's such a love nest."

I said, "I can think of worse."

He looked surprised. "True," he said.

"So did you tell him?" I said.

"What?"

"That we weren't."

Jake coughed. "No. Just said, No, sir, it won't happen again."

"You did?"

"Yep."

I began to laugh.

He laughed too.

"Are you okay?" I asked, moments later.

"Mmmm," he mumbled.

"What's wrong?"

He was ruffling the bristles on his cheeks with his palms, frowning. "I'm just a little dizzy," he said. "Not bad. And my skin is crawling. But not too bad. God. Sometimes I hate myself," he said. "Things are going well, then I do something stupid and screw everything up."

"But it's not screwed up," I said.

"It's not?"

"No, I'd have to say it's completely unscrewed up."

"Completely unscrewed up," he repeated. "That's the opposite of bad?"

"Right."

"So it's good."

"Yes."

He seemed to be savoring this. "Good is a weird word. Almost gross sounding." He started to pronounce *good* in various grotesque voices and accents, which then caused him to retch.

"Jake, are you okay?"

"Mmm."

"Want to lie down here?"

"I'd better go outside," he said.

"Want me to come?"

"I don't think so." With that he did a wobbly little crouch-walk, his knees and arms all tangled and swinging as he attempted to get up. "Damn," he said, grabbing the doorknob, and without looking back he stumbled out of sight.

I sighed.

I stayed awake for a while. I was listening to the internal noises of the dorm. From an upper floor I could hear water running, and someone coughing, and a window slamming shut. From below I heard laughter. I heard a ball bounce. I thought I heard someone howling at the moon. It reminded me of when I'd sleep over at a friend's, and I'd lie awake listening to all the sounds another family made simply going to bed in their own house, and somehow this always made me feel kind of sad.

●

"Man," Jake said, jolting up against the seat belt. "You must think I'm a lightweight. Those mushrooms were, like, putrid."

"No big deal," I said. He'd wake every fifty miles or so, murmur an apology, then nod off again. But I didn't care. I was fine. I felt like I had some elbow room in this day. The highway stretched out before me without any ambiguity. Everything along the way looked even more interesting than it had coming up. The hills covered with oaks, the cows, the dry bed of the underground Salinas River we kept passing over, the oil derricks near Paso Robles, the mission I could see from the road—everything I saw seemed significant. And I liked knowing I'd be making $4 an hour that night, and going straight to work instead of having to stop at home.

Sal had had some delinquents working there in our absence. The place was a disaster. None of the cooking sheets had been cleaned, the floor was covered with flour and bits of cheese, and there was grease all over the front of the cash register.

"So," Jake said. "We're back."

"Yeah."

"And I was thinking, maybe we could do something again sometime."

"Sure," I said.

"I mean, if you're not too busy."

"Sounds good."

"Say it like you mean it!" he said.

"I am!"

"You are?"

And then the crowds started to arrive. Bonfires roared to big blazes on the sand, and we couldn't make enough pizza to keep up. People were ordering whole trays. Unprecedented. Or else ten drinks at once. No time to talk. We'd never been under such pressure before. No sooner did we pull one tray from the oven than we jammed in another. At one point, during a lull, Jake said, "I need a break. I'm still feeling sick." So as it turned out, I ran the place completely by myself for almost forty-five minutes.

It was then that something funny and strange happened which I've never really mentioned to anyone, starting with Jake. Maybe I didn't want him to apologize again. After all, he was the one who took me to Santa Cruz, which changed the course of my life. (Because a letter came a few weeks later informing me I'd be receiving a full tuition grant, work study, and a loan. I would be leaving home in the fall, after all.)

But for the time being, I was running a pizza shack on the beach, and when the back door flew open and a metallic tube rolled across the floor, I barely gave it a thought, until it began to explode into sparks and smoke, thundering through the cement-block cavity like dynamite. Pieces of grit and ash flew into my eyes and I dropped to the floor, blinking and shaking my head.

Well, Sal had warned us. I heard people shouting, but I had a sensitive ear anyway and it sounded as if they were calling from a great distance. "You all right?" I heard. I spit some sand out of my mouth and wiped my eyes, while some customers took the liberty of coming in the back. They were wiping my face with one of our old towels and suggesting I take a trip to the emergency room. After a moment or two, I said no. I said I was fine.

I guess I was fine. My eardrums crackled and my eyes stung, but I got back on my feet and started working. In a few minutes the smoke had cleared and everything was running smoothly again. No one would have guessed there had been a problem. Including Jake. That was the funny part, that when he returned I never mentioned it. Just business as usual. Not a word. I liked him a lot, and always wondered later why I held back. It all could have been so much different.

S.O.S.

The fog was everywhere, in front of the car and behind, in great gusts rising in the headlights, shrouding the streetlamps, and Bart and I were on one of our missions and we were lost. We'd get the names of people with manuscripts from our professors, because they knew who was doing what; then we'd call these people up and ask if they wanted to submit to our journal, and then we'd go on a spree collecting the manuscripts with the car we borrowed from Doug, a guy who used to live on our hall.

"I can't see anything!"

"I know, be careful."

"It's a solid wall," I said.

"Smells like penguins," he said.

We crawled forward, penetrating the fog

as if we were exploring the inside of a mattress. Bart finally let himself out with his flashlight, trying to locate a street sign. He held his arms out like feelers so he wouldn't walk right into one. "Okay, I found something," he called out. "This is Lighthouse. We're just a couple blocks over from Pelton."

He walked ahead of the car. He'd wave the beam when I was supposed to turn, like a signalman on an airport runway. Sometimes he'd flash *short short short, long long long, short short short,* I guess to be funny. I'd see part of his arm or ear suddenly catching the light. Now a hand popped up in the roiling beam, directing me to park.

"So who's this?" he asked, when I joined him on the sidewalk.

"Someone named Carter Berlin."

"Carter Berlin?" His mouth puckered with distaste.

"Yeah, supposedly he has some great prose poems about the fecundity of farm life."

"These people are so pretentious," Bart muttered.

We strutted up the steps and knocked. An older woman in a housecoat, pin curls plastered to her head like limpets, fussed with a stack of locks to find out what we wanted from her.

"Is this where we can find Carter Berlin?" Bart said.

"No, I'm sorry," she said. "He's not here anymore."

I said, "Know when he'll be back?"

She said, "Sometime tomorrow to pick up the rest of his things."

"You mean, he moved out?"

"That's right. We have a little room in back we rent to students, but Carter is no longer with us," she said.

"It must have been sudden, because we just talked to him yesterday," I said.

"Yes, it was very sudden and now he's forfeited his deposit," the woman said.

"Let's leave him a message," Bart said.

"Yeah, tell him to contact *The Blunt Probe*," I said.

"All right." A bulging black handbag sat by the door like a toad. She pulled a little memo pad from one of its folds, the kind of memo pad that had a little loop on the side holding a miniature pencil. "Let me write it down, or I'll forget. Say it again."

"Tell him we're looking for him and we want him to submit something to *The Blunt Probe*," I said, watching her write in her big schoolmarmish hand: *Carter—you must submit to the blunt probe!*

"It's a magazine, so you should capitalize it," I said.

Her hand froze, as if spanked.

"Never mind," I said.

"Thank you," Bart said.

"The room is very clean and the rent is two hundred a month. That includes all utilities, and of course there are kitchen and laundry privileges—" I could see, over her shoulder, the man who completed the picture. He was sporting an enlarged yellow cardigan, and the capillaries of his cheeks were ruddy and bursting, and he was pacing fretfully, as if his world was out of balance because we were at the door.

"Yeah, we'll spread the word," I said.

When we got back in the car, Bart said, "We're screwed. We're past our deadline, and we still don't have anything good."

"So what about *your* stuff?" I said.

"As a fallback," said Bart. "What about the list—anybody else?"

I tried to make it out in the light from the streetlamp, which was moving in whorls through the fog. "Okay, there's a woman in the Soquel hills who's got some shaped poetry," I said.

"What's that?"

"You know, say, a poem about a tree in the shape of a tree, that kind of thing."

"Fuck her," Bart said.

"Why?"

"Who needs it? Why can't we find the next Beckett, the next—did I tell you about Allen Ginsberg?"

"What?" I said.

"Holy shit, I didn't tell you he's coming here?"

"No!"

"He's coming here next month. He's giving a reading downtown. Donald Pickett told me. He asked if I'd write it up for the paper!"

"Wow, I can't believe it!"

"Yeah, I knew you'd be excited."

"More than excited."

Perhaps incongruously, Ginsberg was a hero of mine. What we had in common was just about nothing, but his writings had, over the past few years, worked their way heavily into my consciousness and were the nuts and bolts of my current worldview. My City Lights editions of *Kaddish* and *Howl* were mauled from use, and I'd poured through numerous biographies and accounts of the Beat movement: Kerouac, Cassady, Burroughs, Corso, Ferlinghetti, to name a few. I envied the camaraderie I read about, respected how those people lived their lives around the clock in the name of art. Hardly my style. I had fantasies of myself as a hard-liver, grim and determined, tooling down the road with my cronies and my dreams, but found myself unable to keep it up. It was hard for me to roar and jostle with a roomful of people more than an hour or two. A strange thing would happen. I'd suddenly feel like I was *pretending* to have fun even if I *really* was having fun; then I'd start looking around and wondering the same about everyone else, and it would abruptly seem like we were all as frivolous as decals on an eerie black backdrop of oblivion, and it would wreck everything.

"Did you know Ginsberg's mother was insane, and she was in an institution and had electroshock therapy, and finally he authorized a lobotomy?" I said.

"It's nice when someone's certifiably insane," Bart said.

"How?"

"Because then they can't ruin your life by being *covertly* insane."

I nodded with full understanding. "Hey, ever been to Paterson, New Jersey?"

"Never," Bart said.

"I want to go someday. William Carlos Williams came from there too."

It had been my idea to use Ginsberg's quote from the inside cover of *Kaddish* as an epigram in our magazine—*The established literary quarterlies of my day are bankrupt poetically thru their own hatred, dull ambition, or loudmouthed obtuseness*—and of course we strove to counteract all that by printing the best ditties we could possibly scrounge up from the students and faculty at the school.

"You'll have to come meet him when I interview him," Bart threw in.

"I'll say. You know, maybe we could get some stuff from him," I suggested.

Bart said, "For *our* magazine?"

"Why not?"

"If we get something from him, we'll be made," Bart said. "We'll get funding to keep it going for sure!"

"Yeah!" We then fell into the kind of passionate embrace that we would fall into if Bart was feeling happy, and kissed the way we did when he was happy, so I felt happy, at least I felt the way I did when he felt happy.

We ended up back at my house that evening, first dropping the Datsun back at Doug's, then walking eighteen blocks home through the mist. A Fruit and Nut stand by a lonely highway, enhanced with technicolor to make it look like a destination spot, had found its way onto the face of a postcard that was now waiting for me on the kitchen table. On the writing side there was barely room for a message, because it was cluttered with ancient penny stamps that looked like they'd been peeled from rocks and stumps. In tiny print:

Am driving north to attend a medical conference in SF 3/9. Thought I'd come through and see you. Set me a place at dinner! Looking forward, darling, Your Mumsy.

"Oh, my God," I said to Julie, my roommate, who was chasing the last Cheerio in her bowl. "My mumsy's coming."

"Your what?"

"My mumsy."

"What's that?"

I started laughing hysterically. "It's a grandmother you haven't seen in years because she's schizoid!"

"Seriously?" She looked like she wanted to laugh too but wasn't sure if she should.

"Oh, no!" I said, examining the postcard again.

"What?"

"She's coming the day of the Allen Ginsberg reading. That's going to mess up everything!"

"Well, she'll understand you have a life, won't she?"

"I don't know. Damn."

"Doesn't matter, I'll probably be home. I'll let her in, give her something to eat, administer the tranquilizers."

"You would? That would be swell," I said.

"Sure, don't worry about it," Julie said. She was a rock, the kind of roommate you want to hold on to. We'd been together since freshman year, first in the dorms and now in our own little house off campus. She grew up on a farm in South Dakota, was a biology major, studied a lot, knew how to fix things, and acted like a protective older brother. "How schizo can she be?"

"She's usually benevolent to strangers."

In my room, Bart was already under the covers of my lumpy futon bed. His pants continued to stand in a dwarfish pile exactly where he'd shed them. André Breton's *Manifestoes of Surrealism* poked up from the sheets.

"I have a dilemma," I said.

"What?"

I said, "Okay, I've told you about my grandmother, right?"

"Your grandmother. Dead?"

"No, alive."

"What about her?"

"The crazy one in Santa Barbara?" I coached.

"Yeah, right."

"Well, she's driving through next month, and she's going to stop by."

"She can still drive?"

"She's only in her sixties," I said.

"Is she safe on the road? I mean, being crazy and all."

"She isn't crazy that way. She's twisted and vicious to family members."

"She functions in society."

"Used to," I said. "I mean, I guess she's still a doctor in some capacity. She's on her way to a medical conference. But Roy happens to know one of her neighbors, and they always tell us the latest on how she's becoming really eccentric. Like everyone calls her place the Haunted House of Hope Ranch because it's all overgrown and the shutters are falling off, but then she has these big parties, like she'll meet some guy on an airplane who says he's an Italian count and she'll befriend him and throw him a party, and then people come over and everything's all cobwebs and stuff, and she's wearing these horrible furs and a wig and acting like it's all really elegant even though rats are running up the drapes."

Bart wrinkled his nose. "Episcopalian?"

"Yeah, but, so?"

"Just sounds like the way they bite the dust."

"Anyway, maybe Roy embellishes it to make my mother happy. I don't know if I believe it."

My phone rang. I decided not to tell him about the timing.

"Oh, hi," I said to my mother. I rounded my back to Bart, employing my technique of stretching the phone as far as the cord would allow, until I was sitting cross-legged inside my own closet.

"Hi, dear," she said. "How was your day? Get the package yet?"

"Oh, yeah, I did. Yesterday."

"You were supposed to call!"

"I know, I know," I said. "I was going to. But I have some bizarre news. Guess who's coming."

"Who?"

"Guess."

"I hate guessing."

One thing at a time. "Allen Ginsberg," I said.

"Wait, isn't he one of those poets you like so much?" Mom said.

"Exactly."

"Is he coming to your college to speak?"

"Yeah."

"That's very exciting. I hope you'll get to see him."

"I might get to *meet* him. Oh, and guess who else is coming."

"Who?"

"Dr. Frost," I said.

A silence.

"What does she have to do with Allen Ginsberg?"

"Nothing."

"I don't understand," Mom said.

"She wrote me a postcard and said she's coming," I said.

"You're going to see her?" Mom choked out.

"Well, what can I do?"

"You could not see her," Mom said.

I was sitting in my closet, surrounded by my robe and my clothes and the tips of belts and scarves, peering out at Bart, who was rolling over to look at the clock. This is what he did whenever he was there and Mom called. After a few minutes, he'd start huffing and kicking the sheets around with his feet.

"But maybe, somehow, she's better," I said.

Mom said, "This is unbelievable." She began to wheeze. "It's like you've stabbed me with a knife."

"But why?"

"How—I—how can you entertain the notion of seeing the person who all but ruined my life? Who—who exterminated my self-confidence, who destroyed my aspirations, who—who reduced me to rubble every waking moment of my youth?"

Her voice made me feel dizzy. I was stunned by how I'd miscalculated her reaction. "Mom, I'm not trying to upset you. I mean, she wrote to me out of the blue. What should I do?"

"Do what you want," Mom said, and hung up.

I let out a scream and burst from the closet.

"What's wrong?" Bart said.

"She's mad about my grandmother coming!"

"Get in bed," Bart said.

"I'm too upset," I said, feeling like I might cry.

"She'll get over it."

"No, no, no, you don't understand. This isn't some little thing." I went out to the kitchen and gulped a glass of milk, creating a frigid tunnel near my lungs. I gasped for breath.

Five minutes later, my phone was ringing.

Bart said, "Let's unplug it."

"What good would that do?"

"End the tyranny," he said. "Keep you from being a slave."

I detested Bart right then. For a second I imagined struggling with him at the edge of a cliff.

"You're going to let Dr. Frost visit you?" my sister, Kathy, accused me, when I picked it up.

"Why are you joining in?" I said. "This is sick!"

"It sure is," she said.

"Look, she wrote and said she was coming. It's not like I invited her."

"So you'll just be gone when she comes, right?"

"This is the biggest schism of our lives, don't you understand?"

"How can you do it to Mom? Do you know how upset she is? She's in the bedroom crying!"

"I'm not doing anything to her." Bart started kicking the sheets.

"Then tell her you're not going to see Dr. Frost."

"Don't tell me what to do!" I said.

We both hung up. I was shaking with rage.

"Come on, they're manipulating you," Bart said.

"Hey, don't say that, you're making it worse."

Bart said, "Okay. If you want to stay on the phone all night, I'm leaving."

I shrugged.

"You need to get a little separation going here. You talk to your mother every day!"

"Not every day."

"You act like she drives you crazy, but you're attached at the hip."

I said, "Why should I take your advice? You *never* talk to your family."

"I know what I'm doing, believe me," he said.

I watched with dread as he pulled on his pants and left; then I too let myself out of the house and walked around the block, gulping fog like it was medication for what ailed me. Actually, I didn't know what ailed me. I wondered what was driving me into this battle. After all, I wasn't crazy about seeing Dr. Frost the day of the Ginsberg reading. But her visit seemed important and inevitable, the way an eclipse is known about for years before it occurs. I'd been waiting that long for a breakthrough. Why couldn't anyone understand that?

Back in my room, the phone was already ringing. Mom's voice was phlegmy. She said, "Get to the point. Exactly what do you have in mind?"

"Let's say she stops by," I began. "If she's reasonable, great. If she's creepy and weird, I'll kick her out." Then I tried some handy phrases like *I'll be taking one for the team* and *This is a boil that needs to be lanced.* I was gambling that in the end I'd be seen as a hero. I imagined the reunion and saw the sun coming out from behind the clouds. I saw Mom and Dr. Frost beaming at me, together again, joyous and proud.

"I don't like it," Mom said.

"Why?"

"She's insidious, and she'll most likely say something to create a wedge," Mom said.

"But that won't work!"

"She always causes heartache."

We ended up talking a long time that night. To regain our goodwill we veered from the subject of my grand-mother. Mom wanted to hear the latest about the maga-zine, news of Bart and his studies, if Julie and I had been using the tea towels she'd sent, as well as the special Ger-man lint-removing brush, and an item-by-item appraisal of the latest batch of black sweaters she'd rounded up for me at the local thrift store. Finding stuff for me at the local thrift store, an especially fertile one, was her hobby. "By the way," I said, "I think I'm getting into brown."

"Brown. All right, I'll see what I can find."

"Thanks, Mom."

"Don't forget, it's your grandfather's birthday soon, you should send him a card."

"I already did, Mom."

"My God, I feel sick to my stomach," she said.

"Why?"

"I'm frightened of her—I still have nightmares about her. It's impossible to convey the horror she inspires in me. I think she may have tried to strangle me when I was a baby!"

What could I say to that? "Gee, that's awful."

"Yes, it is."

After we hung up, I couldn't relax. In a while, I called Bart.

"You can come back now," I said.

"What makes you think I want to?" Bart said.

"Just a thought."

"I feel like I should be mad at you, but I'm not sure why," Bart said.

I was tired. "Just come over."

"See you in a minute," Bart said.

We'd been together a year and a half. Until the magazine happened, I'd been hanging by a thread, at least academically. I went to my classes—history, mostly—and listened to the lectures, but never did the required work on time or with much enthusiasm. Occasionally, something would strike my fancy and I'd pour my guts into it, like "The Saga of Wang Tung Ping," which I wrote for a Third World Studies class about the Chinese Cultural Revolution. The assignment was meant to be a ten-page research paper, but "Wang Tung Ping" came in at fifty-five pages. Despite the bibliography, which documented the eighty-seven books and articles I'd used in my research, my professor was annoyed. "Not what I asked for," he wrote. Starting the magazine with Bart was the best thing that had happened in college so far, and what threw us together in the first place.

Bart was from Cleveland, Ohio. His dad was a welder at some company with defense contracts. He probably spent his days blowtorching tanks and bombs, but no one knew. I'd met his family on a trip we took together over Christmas break (Mom was mad I didn't come home, Bart triumphant), and the main thing I'd noticed was that Bart was more annoyed by his own family than he was with mine. He referred frequently to the lifetime prison of their Catholicism, which had placed him, in his youth, at the hands of loathsome nuns. Not a cliché, he declared stoutly. Bart's parents spent a lot of time watching TV in a living room dominated by a large defunct aquarium full of miscellaneous objects, like dog chews and newspapers and a bowling pin and some coffee-stained pink slippers and a plastic bag of yarn knickknacks made by Bart's mom for craft fairs at the church. His dad hardly uttered a word, preferring to glower at everyone coming and going through the door. And his mother seemed nervous and reserved, wearing an apron at all times, even over her nightgown. Portraits of Bart's smiling older twin sisters, champion baton twirlers in their day, proliferated throughout the house, hinting at the era of trophies and saddle shoes the family must have considered its prime.

We spent as little time as possible in their company while visiting, hanging out at the corner tavern and playing pool and catching up with Bart's old friends. Bart's network in Cleveland was vast and multilayered. Friends and their brothers and sisters and second cousins seemed to pop up at the tavern in waves, full of the latest on who'd gotten pregnant, married, or killed in a car crash, and in a way I wondered why Bart wanted to leave it all behind. His sisters were local celebrities. These people's parents had known his. Their grandparents had known his grandparents. Both of us were pretty much anonymous in our seaside town in California.

The first time I saw Bart he was eating alone in the dining hall. I watched him a few nights in a row. He was always eating alone but reading interesting books. One night I sat with him. We played pinball after dinner and he talked about how boring and castrated everybody was. He didn't like anybody, felt superior, and coming from where I did I was used to this kind of person. One thing led to another.

●

Our spirits were high in those days before Ginsberg's visit. For one thing, Carter Berlin turned out to be a master.

We loved his work, especially an epic poem about being a tenant in a neurotic household entitled "Avocado Pig No Fun." It was as honest and real as anything we'd ever published, and, furthermore, he had friends who were busy writing, and now we had things to choose from, and we began to commission artwork, and we planned some readings for our contributors too. Every day turned up some new task that we were more than happy to do.

Spring unfolded early, and that week before the reading I had reason to think this was a place in which I might live forever. (Though I was planning to move to the East Coast after I graduated to find a job at a *real* magazine.) Acacia bloomed all over town, the grass came up soft and scalloped with wild nasturtium, and the sky was a shade of blue so innocent it could have been the color of light before time. Then the day before the reading, everything changed. A warm wind moved in from the west, blew over the clammy ground, and a thick gray mist cloaked the town. You couldn't see what was here. That morning I hid anything in my room that revealed too much about me, picked up a lemon cake at a nearby bakery, filled a bowl with camellias from our front walk, and wrote Dr. Frost a note welcoming her and telling her when I'd be home from the event, which I called "a greatly anticipated encounter with a literary giant." She'd approve.

Julie, who jogged, showered, and finished all her classes every day by noon, said, "Don't forget, I like grandmothers."

"Hope nothing happens to change that," I replied.

In the early afternoon, Bart phoned.

"Hey, can you get ahold of Doug's car?" he asked.

"I can try. Why?"

"Turns out Ginsberg can't do the interview now, but says if I can get him to Bonny Doon tonight, I can interview him in the car and maybe talk some more up there."

"Oh, my God, that would be incredible. Bonny Doon's probably twenty minutes away! We'd be with him for at least twenty minutes!"

"I know. Maybe you should clean out Doug's car," he said. "It's a dump."

"Okay," I said. "Want to help? My grandmother's coming, and I'm kind of nervous."

"She's coming *today*?"

"It's likely."

"You're not going to bring her to the reading, are you?"

"No, of course not."

"Look, I'm up at school now and I've got classes, and then I have to prepare for the interview. Can you manage the car without me?"

"Sure, all right," I said.

"Oh, and don't forget, bring copies of the last few issues, so we can show him what we're doing."

"I will. See you then!" I said.

I was restless. Having this chore would do me good. I made the arrangements with Doug, ran the eighteen blocks over, drove the car back to my place. It was not a prepossessing vehicle, but Ginsberg surely wasn't impressed by material things. All the better, it was an old hulk. The dashboard seemed to be disgorging itself bit by bit, dropping a web of wires and metal boxes and bulbs down onto the place where legs went. The car didn't have power steering, so even though it was a compact, it felt like a tank. You could feel the weight on the tires when you turned. It leaned heavily to the right. I fished many layers of garbage from the floor, discovering hard and moldy things that could not be named: two large trash bags full. Then came the cleaning with a bucket of warm soapy water and a few rags. Every square inch. It was necessary. A previously encrypted stench had been let loose. Every time a car came around the corner, I looked up to see if it was my grandmother. I hurried.

"Ahhhhhh-ooommmmm."
"Ahhhhhh-ooommmmmmmm."
"Ahhhhhh-ooooommmmmmmm."
Ginsberg sat onstage in his suit, holding his harmonium and chanting. I glanced around the room. Barefoot belly dancers in ankle bracelets, men with felted hair and knit caps, babies in papooses, and acidheads young and old seemed to be his local fan base. Literary giant, free spirit: he had all bases covered. After a while, Ginsberg roamed the stage, reading us a new poem about his father's death, and then he sang us a song accompanied by Peter Orlovsky and Bhagavan Das, and then he had us sit in silence awhile to focus on nonthinking. All I could think about was the car ride.

Would Ginsberg acknowledge my humanity without understanding the depth of my feelings for him? Should I try to tell him? Or would that seem insincere and expedient?

Allen Ginsberg would *see* me at least. Bear witness to my corporeal being. I'd probably touch his skin. The eyes that had seen the best minds of his generation *destroyed by madness, starving hysterical naked, dragging themselves through the negro streets at dawn looking for an angry fix* would take me in too, and my image would shoot into his brain and light up some cells and mix with some of the most trenchant thoughts of the twentieth century. My being, otherwise insignificant, would sap some small part of the neurological wonder before me, perhaps elbowing out a great observation he might've made or, far better, nudging into place a notion just on the brink.

After the reading, there followed the usual milling and clumping of the crowd, and Bart went forward to the stage to wait his turn. I saw him rocking on his heels. And shortly Ginsberg smiled his cockeyed smile and Bart smiled his, and they grasped hands and pulled closer and Bart said one thing or another and Ginsberg this or that, and there was nodding and pointing and more talk and gestures, and then Bart was back to me in a flash.

"Quick, go get the car, he'll be coming out the back with his stuff in five minutes," he said.

"Right!" I said.

Alive with purpose, I sprinted out to the street and leaped into Doug's Datsun just as a long black car rolled past, holding a passenger who looked like Julie, furious.

Must have been someone else. Julie was home, and Julie was never furious.

I whipped around the back of the auditorium and drummed my fingers on the wheel. Last-minute inspection—

the smell was subdued, but what was that rubbing sound? I opened the hood, measured the oil, saw that the engine was running on black scum, pulled a couple of cans from the trunk because Doug was never without them, punctured them, poured them, tossed them into the shrubs, wiped my hands on a T-shirt—sorry Doug—and just in time, because the back door of the auditorium swung open and, in a flurry of capes and scarves, Ginsberg's bald pate came into view. He was carrying his harmonium and a little bag.

I was grinning. I felt no gravity in my bones. My hair was clean. I had a good taste in my mouth. I had my whole life ahead of me, and I was already meeting Allen Ginsberg.

Bart introduced us. My palm slid into Ginsberg's warm fleshy palm, then into the cool dry hand of Ginsberg's friend Orlovsky, who grasped his banjo and an ammunition case.

"Greatly obliged," Ginsberg said. "Not the first time I've been interviewed in a car."

A black Town Car pulled around the back of the auditorium. I blinked my eyes. "Please, hop in," I directed them.

"We'll do fine in back," Ginsberg said. It was a two-door, and the men squeezed past the front seats like pears diving into a can.

"Hurry," I muttered to Bart.

"Why? What's wrong?"

"Just get in," I said.

"Don't be weird," he said.

I scrambled to take my seat and start up the car, just as my grandmother and Julie pulled up alongside us. We shot forward abruptly, out of the lot, before Bart had even closed his door. A bellow rang out in our exhaust. A glance in the mirror showed me Julie hurling herself out of the car and jumping up and down, and my grandmother rising from the driver's side, no mistaking her, hollering and waving. Ginsberg and Orlovsky looked startled, tottering over when I pulled onto the street.

"Slow down," Bart said.

"Whoa!" Ginsberg yelped.

"Sorry," I said. "It's—"

I screeched around the corner and bumped over the curb.

"Ann!" Bart yelled.

"Sorry," I said.

Then I took a few unnecessary jags down side streets. Help!

"Cool it," Bart said, squeezing my knee.

"Didn't want the fans catching our scent," I said.

"Ho-ho," Ginsberg said.

Bart fixed me with a glare and then swiveled in his seat, as there were now more important matters to consider. His writing pad and pencil in hand, the interview began. As we motored out of town, through the traffic lights on Mission Street, past the Food Bin, Saturn Café, and Batish House, Bart began to ask the typical questions—about the Jack Kerouac School for Disembodied Poets, at which Ginsberg taught, the effects of marijuana, LSD, and meditation on his poetry, his recent tour with Bob Dylan, his literary influences. It was hard for me to take in the stunning reality of the moment. It was all too much. And what was happening with my grandmother, what was happening to Julie? Was my grandmother reducing her to rubble? Should I have stopped? At last we left the town behind and were heading north on Highway One, a two-lane stretch of road connecting Santa Cruz with San Francisco, between farmlands and the sea, barns and cliffs all obscured now in a thick belt of fog. The man in the backseat could talk about anything and everything like a jukebox you put a dime into for a song. I couldn't help glancing up at my mirror every few seconds. I had it trained on Ginsberg's lips.

A car honked, somewhere nearby. The headlights caught the fog and made flying spumes of it. Lights coming our way blurred into green penumbras and were swallowed up again in the vapor. I slowed to a crawl.

"We have a literary magazine here at school. Ann and I went through a big funding struggle last year," Bart was saying. "It's called *The Blunt Probe.*"

"What does that remind me of?" said Ginsberg.

"Ann?" Bart said.

I cleared my throat. "We were wondering if maybe you'd let us publish something of yours," I said. "It would be a real honor."

"Hmm. I'll see what I can do," Ginsberg said. "Yes, you can give me your address, and I'll look through my notebooks and see what I can do."

"Here's a few back issues," Bart said, handing them over.

"*The Blunt Probe,*" Ginsberg said. *Allen Ginsberg said the name of our magazine!* "It'll look good on my résumé."

We laughed.

"So back to where it all begins," Bart said. "We know what musicians do, practicing their scales, sharpening their technique. What about you? How, exactly, do you do what you do?"

Ginsberg licked his lips. In my mirror I saw it all. "A writer's practice is one of observation. On brick walls, we pick out distinguishing characteristics, the little diagonal slashes in amber and beige which the wisteria find to climb in. Locate particulars, as Wordsworth said, of 'emotion recollected in tranquillity.' Find the vocal origin in your throat that corresponds with the mental image. It's a process of waking up and noticing the ordinary mind. Inspiration—literally, standing open-mouthed to receive the muse—is when you get into your practice of mindfulness for a few hours."

Behind us, a car flashed its lights. In the fog, the brights made it harder still to see.

"Some find that a formal meditation practice, sitting straight spine, helps develop a nonfrenzied mind from which to proceed. Don't be afraid of laziness! Observe and learn from that as well. What's sharp and clear will remain—"

The car behind us began to honk. I moved the mirror off Ginsberg's mouth and found myself squinting into the encroaching glare. In a moment, in a clear pocket between drifting gray curds, I caught a glimpse of the nose of the Town Car.

I bit down on my tongue. The car began to honk again, more frenetically.

"Impatient son of a bitch," Ginsberg said.

Orlovsky twisted around and gave the finger.

"Why don't you pull over when you can," Bart said. "Let them pass."

"Yes, right," I said. I was starting to sweat. When a wide spot appeared, I began to speed up.

"Pull over here," Bart said.

Now she was laying on the horn for seconds at a time, flashing her high beams.

"Maniac," Ginsberg said.

"Do you suppose it's someone trying to tell us something?" Orlovsky said.

"Right here!" Bart said. "Pull over here!"

"I don't want to," I said. "I can't see anything."

The lights flashed into the car and onto the mirror. The horn grew louder and more insistent. The fog was boxing us in, trapping us. "Let's just get to a clear spot," I said.

"Stop the car," Orlovsky said.

"Come on, Ann," Bart said.

"This is monstrous," Ginsberg said.

"We want you to stop," Bart said.

"I can't stop." Tears were mounting in my eyes, ready to spill the banks.

"Why not?" Bart said.

"We have to keep going!" I said.

"Why?"

"Stopping is impossible—"

"No, it's not!"

"It's too dangerous; the road's not wide enough!"

"It's plenty wide enough!"

"We're not going to stop!" I said.

"Stop the car!" Orlovsky yelled.

"Stop telling me to stop!"

The horn was bearing down on us, like the blare of a train. A fuzzy little bunny scurried under the headlights. I swerved onto the shoulder. The shoulder gave way like sponge cake. We went half tilt into a ditch.

"Damn!" Bart said.

I stepped on the gas. We were stuck.

Bart said, "What the hell are you doing?"

"Insanity," Orlovsky said. He struggled against the front seat.

Lights rolled up behind.

Bart reached over and turned the key in the switch. The engine fell quiet. I considered opening the door and running as fast as I could, but he grabbed my wrist before I could try it. "Ann?"

Gravel crunching underfoot.

"Let's see what the jackass wants!" Ginsberg declared.

Knuckles rapping on the glass.

"Open up," she said.

I couldn't move.

Bart said, "Open the window!"

All right, fine. I unrolled the window. My grandmother, whom I had not seen since I was ten years old, stood by the highway. She wore a green paisley blouse, moss-green pants, a gray sweater vest and had her white hair up in a stylish bun.

"That's quite a welcome!" she said. "Get out of this car and give me a hug!"

Bart said, "Gentlemen, I can promise you this was not in the plans."

Ginsberg said, "The plans are not always clear."

I opened my door and stood on the gravel shoulder with my grandmother. "My, how you've grown," she said. "You look just like I did at your age. You've got the red in your hair from Mother. I have a beautiful sweater for you in the car from Scotland. Went over there last year to study. Spent a month in Edinburgh. Bought you a gorgeous kilt too. Come on now, let's get back and have some dinner!"

I hugged her. Tears spilled down my cheeks.

Bart stood on the other side of the car.

"Madam, do you realize you almost ran us off the road?" Ginsberg called out from the backseat.

"Um, this is my friend Bart," I told her, "and in back, this is the great poet Allen Ginsberg and his friend, Peter Orlovsky."

My grandmother bent over and took a quick look. "I don't care if they're Tweedledum and Tweedledee, let's go! I didn't drive up here to chase you all over kingdom come!"

The rest folds in on itself, like a moment you don't quite want to remember. I recall Bart pulling me away by the sleeve and saying, "Tell her to go back to your place and wait!"

"It's okay," I said.

"You're supposed to take pictures!"

"You can take pictures."

"And you've been looking forward to this for weeks," he said. "If you give it up, you're sacrificing yourself for *nothing*!"

"No, no, it's not for nothing."

Then there was Julie. "Sorry," she was whispering. "I'll tell you what happened later."

I'm the one who's sorry, I'm sure I must have said.

And then Bart was saying something like, "You're making a huge mistake."

"No, I'm not."

"You're making a huge mistake in terms of *us*," I think he said.

At that moment I considered him the meanest, most horrible person I'd ever met, and I grabbed my bag from the car and breathed one last time the scent of cloves and old wool that had accompanied the men, and asked for Ginsberg's signature on the only piece of paper I could find, the back of my driver's license. *Ahhhh*, he wrote. *Allen Ginsberg*. What a generous person. Then my grandmother and Julie and I scuffed through the highway gravel back to my grandmother's car. "This is Duke," she said, rapping on the hood of her vehicle. I took my place in the front seat of Duke. Julie flopped in back. The Doctor turned her car around, and we made our return through the marine layer to town.

While we prepared dinner, Julie whispered that she'd never encountered anyone with so forceful a personality. I concurred. I joylessly cooked spaghetti and meatballs for the occasion, while Dr. Frost brought in her bag and her gifts, which included a large bottle of Jack Daniel's. She poured it freely and said it was medicinal. Now, quite clearly, I could see that Bart was right, that I was a pawn, a toad, a scab, and a fool. I'd write a mournful self-hating poem about it soon, which would culminate in the line *Birdbath enzymes digest me make me part of your perfect order!* But I didn't know how to deal with it yet. That evening we sat listening to stories about my grandmother's recent adventures as a physician. She was giddy as a birthday girl, telling tales of millionaires who'd proposed to her, honors she'd been presented with, famous people she'd met along the way. My least favorite was the one about her rotations at Harbor Hospital and how aroused the men were at the sight of her, their erections stirring under the sheets "like prairie dogs in the grass," she told us.

"Say," she said, after Julie went to bed, "I want to take the mail boat up the west coast of Norway this summer. It's a fabulous trip. I want you to come with me."

"This summer?" I said. "Thank you for the offer, but I've already got plans."

"Change your plans. This is a once-in-a-lifetime opportunity. It's a real mail boat. It stops in every little fjord! We'll have a ball!"

"Mumsy," I said, tasting the old name on my tongue, "I would love to, but I'm graduating in a couple of months, and then I'm probably driving back east this summer. I want to try to get a job at a magazine, either in New York or Boston."

"Well, good for you. But take a little vacation with me first!"

Even if I wanted to go to Norway, how could I, with my

mother feeling as she did? I'd have to go secretly. It would be like having an affair—with my grandmother. "Thanks, it sounds great, but I think I'm going to need to dig in and start looking. I don't know anybody out there."

"That's no way to look for a job. You've got to know somebody! You get yourself one beautiful suit, linen is best, and a simple strand of pearls. Get a studio apartment and go join a club. Try the Junior League or the Commonwealth Club. Make a few friends in high places. Let 'em know who you are and what you're there for. Always look your best. Pretty soon you'll get a lead. Always write thank-you notes. If the lead turns out to be a dead end, don't quit!"

"Great advice, Mumsy," I said.

"But first let's take a trip up the coast of Norway."

"Well, we'll see."

"Remember that trip we took together, years ago?" she said. "It was wonderful. You were a delight to travel with."

"Me? A delight?"

"You bet," she said.

"I remember that man you met there," I said.

"What man?"

"You don't recall a certain Dr. Von Allsberg?"

"Oh, him," she said. "Turned out to be a snake."

"Remember Mom?" I said, surprising myself.

"My only daughter? Yes, I remember her," she said.

"Too bad you guys lost touch," I said.

"Yes, too bad."

"I think she really misses you," I said.

"Mmm. That's hard to believe," she said, and I tried to hide my blush.

"No luxury," she continued on the next morning, over our bowls of oatmeal. "You'd never catch me on one of those ersatz cruises. This is a real mail boat! At every port you get off and explore. You eat regular grub with the crew and have a functional little room, all very authentic."

I helped her put her bags in the back of the Town Car, as she had to be in San Francisco by noon. The fog was so dense, I was afraid she might postpone her departure. But it was nothing to her. "Listen, darling, I'm putting down a deposit next week," she told me.

"There's something I really don't like about mail boats," I insisted.

"How do you know? Ever been on one?"

"And I don't think I like delivering things in fjords," I said.

"Why? What's wrong with fjords? Oh, you're pulling my leg! It's going to be a fantastic trip," she said, and as she gave me a kiss and vanished in the mist, I was certain right then I'd be moving across the country soon, saying goodbye to every piece of this.

The Possible World

It was strangely quiet outside, but maybe I had closed all the windows. This was the most well-built house I had ever lived in. The walls were creamy plaster, like those in an adobe mission. They were held together by strong oak beams, which were exposed like whale ribs across the living room ceiling. Even the windows were made of a thicker, more interesting glass than normal windows. Tiny bubbles riddled the panes if you looked closely enough. For some reason I liked to walk around this house and examine its craftsmanship. Someone who appreciated a well-built house built this one.

I was only a renter. This house would probably cost some unreal amount. Though well built, it's small. And the person I married, who is a software engineer over in San Jose, thinks only of owning big, cumbersome things. In them, I see nothing but trouble.

Anyway, it was suddenly quiet, and though I could see the trees whipping around in the wind, I couldn't hear a single groan or rustle. It was a soothing but rather apocalyptic feeling. I had a hunch I would not be staying in this house much longer.

Yesterday Paul, who is my landlady's boyfriend, called at exactly this time. It was 9:30 A.M., and I was already watching a movie on TV. He said, "I need some help on the brocco-rabi project. As you know, I broke my leg daredevil skiing and I need someone to drive me to Stockton to inspect the site of our first brocco-rabi demonstration. Can you drive me? A hundred dollars?"

This isn't exactly what he said verbatim, but all of this was there. And even though it was an abrupt request, I was strangely happy about it. I didn't have anything special to do yesterday before picking up my son from his preschool. A drive to Stockton sounded out of the ordinary.

"Okay," I replied. "If I can find a way for Will to be picked up and taken care of, I'll do it."

"Yeah, I've got that all figured out already," Paul said. "Virginia will be done with her meetings by then. She can pick him up."

Virginia is my landlady. It's hard to ignore how much she likes my son. On Easter she dropped by a basket with Godiva eggs in it. Plus an expensive, plush stuffed rabbit. It made me a little uncomfortable. Then on Halloween she made up a grab bag of candy and toys, very extravagant. Twice she'd asked me to bring him over and they'd baked cookies together. The kind of thing he'd have done with his grandmother, if she lived nearby and were still alive.

Yesterday it was windy like today. I was to pick Paul up *asap,* whatever that meant. I decided to take my time with my cup of coffee and my movie, seeing as he'd given me such short notice. But even so I could tell I was hurrying a little. This movie seemed like a strange choice for the morning, before the day had left its scratchy imprint on a person. A respectable businessman takes his daughter and son into the outback of Australia, tries to kill them, sets the car on fire, and shoots himself in the head. Rambling across the desolate expanse, they meet an aboriginal boy on walkabout, the year he's learning the skills necessary for survival. He shows them how to eat grubs, swim naked in a pool. They pick up a thing or two. When they return to civilization, nothing can ever be as harsh. Or can it?

Before Paul called, I hadn't really been sure of my plans for the day. Probably the library, the laundry, the bank. Not much to get excited about.

But I've really got to stop doing that, shortchanging my plans like that. Lots of other significant things could've happened. I might've had an interesting idea that I could jot down in a notebook, for future use somehow. Or maybe I'd receive a phone call with news that would distract me for a day or two.

Two weeks ago, my sister, who now lives in New York and calls me quite often, arranged for the largest radio station in her area to call and interview me. She loves to imagine me back in the swing of things, and my involvement with brocco-rabi had given her fresh hope. She called the radio station to see if they were interested, and they were. Hard to believe. When I don't care, not invested at all, I'm in demand. Anyway, she told them I was the person to talk to when it came to brocco-rabi. The radio station contacted me, and before I knew it I was scheduled to go on the air. It's a 50,000-watt radio station. It can be heard from Maine to South Carolina.

The thing is, I'm not really the person to talk to about brocco-rabi. But my sister was so excited to have put together this interview that I had to go along with it.

The host of this show was a man named Newt Barnaby. About five minutes before two, an assistant called. "Ready for Newt?" she asked. I said I was. I had practiced speaking with more authority the night before. I thought I should sound like the world's expert on brocco-rabi.

Suddenly I could hear the actual radio show coming through the phone—a commercial for a car wash. I sighed. Ultimately, nothing was resting on this. No one but my sister would hear it. If Virginia and Paul found out, they'd probably be irritated. Here I was, posing as the official spokesperson for brocco-rabi. Just then the voice of Newt Barnaby began to talk over the end of the car wash ad. My throat tightened up.

"And now we've got a very interesting feature for you today. Out in Salinas, California, a brand-new vegetable is on the loose, and we've got Ann Ransom to tell us about it!"

"Hi, Newt," I said jauntily.

"Ann! How's it going out in Salinas?"

"Actually, I'm not in Salinas. I live in Aptos." Why did I need to throw that in? Who cared? I concentrated harder.

"Where's Aptos?"

"Near Watsonville. This is a vast agricultural area, Newt. The Pajaro and Salinas valleys are among the richest growing areas on earth."

"Lucky you! We Easterners know the good veggies always seem to come from California. So tell us—what exactly is brocco-rabi?"

I was doing better now. My voice was coming on strong and clear.

"Well, Newt, brocco-rabi was genetically engineered. As you can probably guess, it's half broccoli and half kohlrabi. It's a hearty grower and has five times the vitamins of both combined. It's quite large and looks kind of like a big green cow udder."

"Yeow! The Frankenstein of vegetables!" Newt Barnaby emitted a resounding, fully committed laugh. And I smiled. I was staring out the thick, bubbly window into the backyard. From the inside of this house, the outside had never looked more interesting.

"Yes, and it's the first new vegetable to be created since 1937, when scientists masterminded the Brussels sprout."

"Really! Ann, this is absolutely fascinating."

Did he really think so? I was afraid I had my dates wrong, and surely some know-it-all would call the station to correct me. Better get back on firm ground.

"Furthermore, we're about to introduce Chucky Brocco-rabi, a larger-than-life superhero. He wears a cape and a little bikini like most of the other superheroes do—"

"Ho-ho. Tell us, does brocco-rabi taste good?"

"Sure. Everybody loves it."

"Where can I find brocco-rabi? Can I drive over to Price Chopper and buy some right now?"

"I certainly hope so. We believe it's now in every state, and it's catching on in Europe too."

"What's the bottom line on brocco-rabi, Ann? Why should America open its heart to a new vegetable?"

"Newt, what with the government's five-a-day plan, we need all the options we can get at the lunch and dinner table. Kids are really going to love brocco-rabi too. The weirdness of it."

"Weird! Weird! I love it! Thanks: Ann Ransom from Aptos, California!"

Newt disappeared and all the sound collapsed into a vacuum in the phone. I was afraid my eardrum would be sucked in too. That was it? No goodbyes? I was suddenly alone again in my kitchen, looking down at the soaking skillet from the wild rice dish I'd prepared the night before. I slowly hung up the phone. Then, a moment later, my sister called. She said I sounded like a natural. She said she was sure brocco-rabi sales would skyrocket.

Later, I thought it was kind of foolish for me to have gotten so worked up about this radio interview, broadcast over states where nobody I knew would be listening.

Anyway, yesterday I vacuumed the car before I drove to

pick up Paul. I sprayed some room freshener in it and packed up a tin of cookies. Then I went and filled the tank with gas and squeegeed the windows. For some reason I wanted to do a really good job of driving Paul to Stockton. I admit I was overly excited about this trip.

As I've said, it was windy yesterday. But I like weather. It's one of the few things that can make everything seem different when you're in exactly the same place.

●

The person I married thinks Paul is something of a blowhard, but he likes him. One day, shortly after we'd met and moved into this house, the air was clear and bright and he had the day off. He planned on doing a little lawn mowing, making himself a martini, then lying out on a chaise in the freshly threshed grass. He doesn't get to enjoy our yard often and wasn't even aware, until that day, that I had planted an extensive summer garden that had provided us with most of our salad materials recently. At any rate, he had only just turned off the roaring two-horsepower engine on the mower when Paul showed up with a box of wires and switches.

"Hey, buddy," Paul said, "I need to put lights down in the crawl space, and even though I'm an aeronautical engineer I know a hell of a lot about electronics and you can come down there and shoot the shit with me."

This wasn't exactly what he said, but if you read between the lines it was clear this was his meaning. And even though this person never does anything he doesn't want to do, he put aside his martini and chaise and disappeared into the basement crawl space with Paul for the rest of the afternoon. Then that night he was amazed at himself.

"Why did I spend my afternoon off crawling on my belly in the dirt?" he asked me.

"I was wondering. What did you talk about all that time?"

"He insisted on installing five different switches and bulb outlets. Two would have been more than enough. That Paul is pretty proud of himself. Was some kind of boy genius. Did some engineering contracts for the military and spent a year in a tunnel under Saudi Arabia. Said they had golf courses down there."

"Golf courses? How deep were the tunnels?"

"I think he said two miles."

"Two miles deep. Amazing! Golf courses!"

"I don't know. Maybe I wasn't listening."

"Not listening? It really sounds much more interesting than I expected."

In fact, as the afternoon wore on, I had crawled over to the heavy scrolled wrought-iron heater vent and pressed my ear to it. I stayed there for a long time, trying to hear the sound of their voices. The smell of moist soil came up through the vent in gentle waves. It made my mouth water. Sometimes I heard a roar like the ocean, and for a while I heard scratching like a squirrel making a nest. But that's it. I guess it's such a well-built house, sound doesn't travel. I determined I wasn't missing much.

"Well, maybe he feels at home down there," I said, wondering why I wanted to prolong this discussion.

"Who?"

"Paul."

"Where?"

"Under the house. Maybe it reminds him of Saudi Arabia."

"Oh, right. Let's hope he doesn't decide to put a golf course down there," my husband said.

It pleased me to see him interacting with someone, if that's what it was. He seemed to have few friends and worked forty-five miles from our house. Only once had I gone to his office, and that was to take him his briefcase, which he had forgotten. When I found him there, he seemed glad to see the briefcase but asked me to speak quietly, and I remember how we ended up talking in whispers. I had already realized I was married to someone who didn't like the sound of the human voice. Raised an only child by old, quiet parents, he couldn't help it, but this was the truth about him. Say I started speaking in the yard to a neighbor over the fence. He would come out on the porch and stare. If I were on the phone laughing, he would walk into the room with a funny look on his face. That's the way he was. To talk to someone all afternoon in the moist soil under the house meant he liked him. I wanted him to like someone.

So yesterday Paul descended from Virginia's house in his full leg cast. I leaped from my car and offered to help him in. "I've got it, Ann," he said. "Thanks." Like an excellent chauffeur I opened the passenger door for him. "So, thanks for hopping to on such short notice," he said. "You're a trouper. Besides, I know you didn't have anything else to do today."

Of course, he really said something else, but I knew what he was thinking. Paul and Virginia specialized in promotions. After we moved into their house and they found out that I had done some editorial work in the past, they offered me jobs from time to time. I never asked for them and often wondered how they knew I would say yes. I guess because I lived in Virginia's rental I imagined they could see me rattling around inside it. So I spent a few days coming up with names for a new organic shampoo that would be sold pyramid style, by couples working their own neighborhoods like hungry coyotes. Then, a couple months ago, Paul and Virginia wangled the brocco-rabi account, a fairly sizable one, I gathered, and I started taking on assignments regularly. There were press releases and so forth. And then this grand opening for Chucky came up. I'd been on the phone to all kinds of official people in Stockton for the past month. The actual event was now only a few weeks away. And yet even though I'd tagged along with Paul and Virginia on meetings with N & B, and attended all the planning for the commercial that would be made during the event with the video people, I couldn't help worrying that this might not be the best way to market brocco-rabi. Get the kids excited by brocco-rabi and they'll bug their mothers into buying it; that was the cornerstone of their strategy. They had created 3-D cartoon activity books all about Chucky and planned to bring Chucky into the schools. But I already knew there was nothing lovable about Chucky Brocco-rabi. He had no personality. He couldn't even talk, that was the bottom line. A costume designer was preparing a dozen of the mute green getups at this very moment. Paul and Virginia were spending a lot of other people's money on this. They had their own business, but they didn't have any kids. How could they know?

Paul and I drove the two-lane highway to Stockton. The hills were golden and so was the sky, filled as it was with crop dustings and smog and embers from a fire put out near Paso Robles only the day before. The wind had whipped that fire, then moved up here. It was whipping my car. "I hope Virginia doesn't wimp out on me," Paul said. "I mean, she's the most intelligent woman I know, and yet she's utterly insecure. I need to help her get over it. Same problem destroyed my first marriage. I was off overseas all the time on high-security missions, and so finally to make her feel competent I bought my wife a store."

"A store?" I said. "That was nice of you."

"Yeah, well, it didn't work. After a while she didn't think she could handle it."

"What kind of store was it?"

"Needlecraft, stuff like that. She was an expert at needlecraft."

"Just because she was a needlecraft expert doesn't mean she could run a needlecraft store," I offered.

"She lost her confidence. Tried to kill herself with knitting needles."

"Is that a joke?" I asked.

"If you think that's a joke you've got a strange sense of humor," Paul said.

There was something about Paul that bothered me, I decided.

"It's a tragedy when someone underestimates their talents. By the way, are you aware of how smart your son is?"

"Of course I am," I said. Will was smart, no doubt about it. He started reading when he was four, almost like spontaneous combustion. Not only that, he could identify all the states by shape when he was only two. He had memorized them all on his own.

"I just hope you realize how smart he is. It would be terrible if you didn't." This irritated me for some reason, so I didn't reply. I didn't need to. After all, I was driving and had to be vigilant because cars were speeding and passing. Paul kept blabbing about the uncertain future of Will's intellect while I guarded our lives.

The supermarket we had chosen for this event was on the outskirts of town, in a new suburban area full of cul-de-sacs and shopping centers that had only been in existence for a year or two. The suburb still touched on original almond orchards, full of flowers in the springtime, gray as ghosts by Thanksgiving.

We entered the store and inspected the produce department to make sure it was suitable as a backdrop for both the commercial and the event itself. And it was. It was actually an especially good produce section. Vegetables of every color and shape, fresh and waxy, filled enormous rough-hewn bins that were spotlighted from above. Automatic sprayers jetted over never-dehydrating greens in tiers along the mirrored walls. Paul and I nodded at each other with approval. A quick talk with the produce manager assured us of his cooperation on the day of the event. "He's going to be a phenomenon," Paul bragged to the produce manager, showing him a blueprint of Chucky. "As big as the California Raisins, as big as Joe Camel. We've got a serious budget to play with here. So if you display our product prominently, we can do all kinds of great things for you."

I started to feel sucked in. Paul's droning voice began to compel me to think I was on an important mission. I could tell I was beaming as the produce manager listened and was impressed. At last, completely satisfied, we took off for destination two, the suburban junior high.

"Good work," Paul said.

"Thanks. You too," I added.

At the junior high we met with the leader of the drill team. Two hundred girls were quickly promised to be at our disposal for the event. We would have them do a few routines, substituting Chucky's name for the name of their junior high. This drill team was the top-placing team in the state. We would make a generous contribution to their travel budget. Paul and the drill team leader fawned over each other as they closed the mutually beneficial deal. Then, as the drill team leader went on a little too long about the special routines her special core squad could do, and the baton twirling that would add to Chucky's luster, I could see the gulf of Paul's insincerity widening. I could tell he didn't like her.

We finished off in Stockton by visiting the chamber of

commerce. There we picked up more endorsements for Chucky and the event. Promises of publicity and even the possibility of a cameo by the mayor. Too much. The truth is, I seem to love being included on other people's missions. This trip was lightening my spirits. As we walked out to my car we gave each other a high five. Paul was bubbling.

"I'll actually spend a few dollars on you to thank you," Paul nearly said. "Let's go over to the restaurant at that big hotel downtown. Okay?"

"Great," I said. I looked at my watch. All that accomplished, and it was still only three o'clock.

"Virginia's probably got Will by now," Paul mused.

"True," I said.

"That's nice. For Virginia. She really wants kids."

I parked in the garage under the hotel. I helped Paul get out of the car and he limped beside me into the lobby. The restaurant was closed between lunch and dinner, so we sat in the bar. Paul ordered an Irish coffee, which sounded exactly right to me, so I ordered one too.

"This is good," I said when it came.

"Want anything off the bar menu?"

"Umm—well, I guess crab cakes."

"Virginia will be incredibly psyched about this," Paul said. "It's all working out. Now all I need to do is contact that reporter from the *Bee* and then the radio station. You want to take care of that?"

"Sure," I said.

And then I'll show Virginia the results and she'll think I did all the work, and she won't resent having to support me, seemed to be what he was thinking. "Miss, can we have a kettle of clam chowder and an order of crab cakes?"

"You know," I said, "I think this is going to be a lot of fun. I think a lot of people will come. That was a great idea you had, about raffling the Rollerblades."

Paul nodded in complete agreement. "The main thing to remember, though, is that the commercial is the most important aspect of the event. So as long as the video people get all the shots they need, it doesn't matter if things don't go perfectly smooth. Doesn't that take a load off your mind?"

"You mean, since I'm the coordinator?"

"Right. Can I ask you a question, Ann?"

"Okay."

"Do you think Virginia is attractive?"

I had thought he was going to ask me if I was a happy, fulfilled person—something that would put me on the spot but make me feel like I had an interesting secret. "Sure," I said sullenly.

"I mean, is she what another woman would call a beautiful woman?"

"Yes, I guess so," I said. I pictured Virginia. She was tall and gangly and cut her red hair like a helmet. I suppose you can say anyone is beautiful, really.

"Do you mind if I tell her you said that?"

"But it's not as if I said, 'Virginia's beautiful' out of the blue."

"But you think so."

Who wanted to argue over something like that? "Yeah, sure, whatever."

Paul smiled at me. It was the first time I could remember him attempting to look pleasant for my benefit. Foolishly, I had looked forward to some new company today in the form of Paul. But try as I might, I didn't have a sense of us connecting.

The crab cakes came, and at least they were good. Paul dipped into his clam kettle. "Chow down," he said.

"Yeah," I said.

"Did you know Virginia wanted to write a postcard to Letterman about Will?" Paul slurped. "Get him on the show."

"What?"

"That state thing. The way he bites Fig Newtons into the shapes of states? That's incredible."

I laughed. "He did that for you guys?"

"Virginia was in shock. I tell you, she's a little bit in love with your son. Who wouldn't be, he's a great kid. But the truth is, we've actually talked about taking care of him if anything ever happened to you and your husband. I mean, we'd go the whole way. We'd adopt him."

I looked at Paul quizzically. "You mean, if both of us died?"

"We're not going to adopt him if you're still alive, obviously."

"You mean you imagined us being dead?"

"All I'm saying is that we would like to volunteer to be the ones who would take care of Will if anything ever happened. That's all."

I slumped in my seat. Never before had anyone discussed the possibility of my own death with me. It felt intimate and indifferent at the same time. As if someone had stripped me of my clothes but not stopped to look. A real insult.

"Let me get this right. You and Virginia were sitting around one day, maybe talking about how nice it would be to have children, and then one of you said something like, 'That Will boy over at our rental is pretty nice,' and the other one said, 'Maybe our tenants will die suddenly and we can have him'?"

"Of course not," Paul said. "Virginia and I put a lot of thought into this."

"And anyway, even if we did die, what makes you think we'd want you two? I have a sister! I have friends!"

"Forget I said anything."

"No, no, I'm glad you told me," I said. "Because, you know, the idea makes my blood curdle."

"Oh, come on," Paul said. "You're overreacting!"

"Yes. It makes me feel really sick, like the crab cakes are trying to crawl out of my stomach."

"You're funny," Paul said, smiling the way he did at the drill team leader. "Virginia and I really appreciate that in your work."

I excused myself. I was really bent out of shape. I needed to ask my husband to go pick up Will at Virginia's house right away. But when I reached his office they told me he had already left. Then I called home. "What happened?" he shouted. "The school called me at work. *At work!* No one ever came to pick up Will. One of the teachers had to sit there waiting with him until I got there."

"Virginia didn't get him? She forgot about him?"

"If I had been out of the office today, what would have

happened? It took me an hour and a half to get there because of traffic, which I always avoid by leaving later."

I said, "You know what? It's just as well, because I'm not going to be working for Paul and Virginia anymore."

"Why on earth would it be just as well?"

"I'm not going to be working for Paul and Virginia anymore," I said again. "Don't you want to hear why?"

"Someone better explain something," he really said. "How would you like to be left at school? My mother never did that to me."

On the long drive back to Aptos, the wind wrestled the car and the passers passed and the sun went down right before our narrowing eyes. Sometimes the road vanished into a dwarfed sunburst on the windshield, and Paul gasped and dug into the floor with his bad leg. I hoped his hair would turn white. I was having trouble dealing with certain people, it was clear. Take, for example, people who thought you could sell a stenchful vegetable by dressing it in a costume, and people who made love to their wives with their shoes on. Last night I crawled out of bed, stretched out flat on the living room floor, and closed my eyes. I imagined traveling to a place where I started over with nothing but my child. I don't know why that scenario always appealed to me so much, but it was the only thing I could think of that carried me through the night.

Last of Our Tribe

One morning, like every morning, I walked my son to the corner to catch the bus for school. And then I just kept on going. I have to emphasize how uncharacteristic this was. I am not the type you see engaged in solo activities, jogging by or cycling up an incline. My pattern at that time was to struggle out of bed after pushing the snooze alarm three or four times and to throw a sweater on over my pajamas, fixing Will eggs and toast and dressing him, though not quite awake when he told me his dreams. After he took off in the school bus I'd walk quickly home and climb back into bed. I didn't sleep the day away, however. Like a schoolgirl sneaking out for a smoke, I just liked knowing I could get away with those few extra moments unaccounted for in my room.

That day I simply didn't feel like turning back. For one thing, I was having second thoughts about where we lived. It was poorly constructed, the part we lived in barely resembling a house. We had to climb forty shoddy wooden steps from the street to enter a side door next to a bare hill of mud, into a laundry room with cement slab floors, adjacent to an ancient Formica counter and a half-sized refrigerator that posed as a kitchen, before turning a corner and finding ourselves in either of two small bedrooms that looked down through the telephone wires at the street. We didn't have a living room or any other rooms. Those were all upstairs. In other words, we lived on the bottom floor of a large ungainly structure that was built on an eroding hillside. The kind that folds up like a house of cards if there's a lot of rain or an earthquake.

Because I lived in a house that didn't resemble one, I noticed that I had started to feel somewhat less real myself. When we moved in, I thought I was a full standing member of the community, but by now I was starting to slouch around in the grocery store like a bottom-feeder. It wasn't easy for Will to invite friends over, because there was no backyard or jungle gym. I couldn't grow a garden on the dissolving hillside. I hated bringing groceries home and carrying them up the forty steps, especially if I had more than two bags. But it was hard to find places in this town. I really couldn't complain.

It was a small beach town in central California called Rio del Mar. Will and I liked walking along the shore, pretending we were California Indians pushed to the edge of the continent. The rest of our kind had long ago been wiped out. We were the only two left. We had to find clever ways to survive. Anthropologists from Berkeley wanted to collect us and study our language, but so far we'd kept them at bay. We knew they wanted to put us in pants that were too short for us, publish books full of our secrets. We knew we didn't want to end up that way.

After I walked another hour or so, it struck me that I'd really blown a fuse. I didn't have a watch on, but I sensed how much time had passed since I'd said goodbye to Will. The sun was now high and bright, the birds taking wider circles in the sky. I began to wonder when I would stop and decide to turn around, and why a simple walk felt like something illicit. Yet I felt compelled to keep going in spite of my day's plans, which included some typing I did for a few employers, some errands, and throwing the ingredients for beef stew into an electric crock.

I was good at humoring people, I thought, as I trudged through the sand. But it took its toll.

Last month my sister and her boyfriend paid us a visit from New York. My sister does modern dance, the real thing, her body as taut as a rifle. Her boyfriend is a statistics professor at NYU. Why they were coming I hadn't been sure, considering how little they see of value in our life out here. To make it worse, the second day of their visit I was told by my landlord I had an hour to remove everything from our false kitchen and hide it so it didn't look like we used it as a "real" kitchen. The inspectors were coming. Our whole arrangement depended on this. We could be evicted. The so-called kitchen was only there to make the bottom floor a separate unit and was not up to code. Some former tenant with a grudge had tattled. So my landlord, a melancholy Chinese man by the name of Jiao, had been plagued by surprise inspections ever since.

We had to act fast. My sister and I ran with our arms full of canned goods back and forth to the bedroom closets, and I filled up bags with food from the refrigerator, and she stacked dishes, even the dirty ones, into a big box, and then the statistics professor helped me lug the boxes out around the back of the house onto the muddy slope. All the while, Jiao was removing the rice-paper wall by the main stairs so that it looked like we all shared the real kitchen and lived together in one happy group.

"Couldn't you find somewhere else to live?" my sister groused.

Stuffing kitchen things under my bed, I came upon a packet of photos from a time Will and I went to visit her. Will was a bald smiling baby then. My sister looked pretty, as usual. Her blond hair was longer, shiny and thick like a cascade of honey coming out of a beehive. Even as I was visiting, she accused me of never visiting, and I remembered how we had a rare quarrel.

"Next thing I know, we'll find you living in a chicken coop," she said to me now.

"What a great idea," I said.

At that moment Jiao stuck in his head. "They are here," he whispered.

The whole time the inspectors were inspecting, my sister and the statistics professor stood huddled together looking guiltier than criminals. I don't think they'd ever done anything fishy between them in their lives. My sister thought our childhood was a Norman Rockwell painting, and the statistics professor was as colorless as a root from spending all his time in dark old buildings chiseling out figures. When the inspectors looked in on them, my sister and the statistics professor turned bright red.

"Nice day," the man with the clipboard said.

"We're just visiting," the statistics professor said.

One night, soon after I moved back to this area, my sister and I both happened to watch a documentary about wolves. We talk a lot on the phone since our mother died, and chatting away we discovered the coincidence the next day. These wolves lived just like families as we knew them. The female wolf would send her man off to hunt, while she stayed home and took care of the children, giving them miniature lessons in hunting and warren-keeping until the father wolf came home at the end of the day. At that time, she would be so overjoyed to see him that she would begin to quaver. She would wag her tail so hard her whole body wagged too. She was quavering and wagging her body around and around her mate, unable to conceal her joy at seeing him again. That, my sister told me, was how she wanted to feel about the next man in her life.

It was an unusually good conversation. I had wanted to feel like a wagging, quavering wolf about someone someday too. At the time I was distracted with figuring out what I was doing here, but I still had a few old contacts and felt relatively at ease. I liked the sound the leaves and bushes made when a storm was coming in from the sea. Like they were shivering and quaking in advance of something special. I liked how long a day could seem when the weather was changing.

I had an odd habit in those first few months. I would drive downtown, park in a garage, then discover I was afraid to get out of my car. You'd think I'd not bother going downtown anymore, but I was optimistic that the problem would resolve itself and I would sit in the yellow light of the parking structure, listening to other car doors open and close, to the cries of young children pulled too hard by the arms, to radios suddenly snapping off and leaving the place quiet again for a moment or two.

And finally one day I managed it. Something propelled me from the car that day, perhaps the feel of a warm breeze scented with fish and madrone or maybe because I was still feeling charged up from that wolf-conversation I'd had with my sister. Anyway, I sat in a café with a notebook and started to jot down some thoughts. A man with a laptop before they were widely available smiled at me from across the room. He had long black hair and a big walrus mustache and it occurred to me that he was exactly my age, though it becomes harder and harder to tell. I smiled back and he made a beeline to my table.

"Whatcha working on?" he asked. "I saw you scribbling like crazy a few minutes ago."

"Me?" I didn't remember scribbling anything, but when I opened my notebook I saw that I had drawn a big tree. It was childish and the ballpoint of my pen had punctured the paper in several places, and an ugly blue tree in a lonely person's notebook was not something to be proud of. "Funny," I said. "I have a habit of doing that when I think."

"And what were you thinking about?"

"One thing I like to think about," I said, not hesitating at all, "is the series of events that led me to this spot, going back as many generations as I can hold in my head. I place everything in its historical context, of course, but I also try to figure out what kind of neurotic personal decisions my ancestors made too. Like stubborn qualities or perverse instincts that caused chain reactions and confusion and misery. Mistakes they made when they married, and so on. Does this make any sense?"

He nodded. "And then you draw family trees," he said.

I looked at my awful picture again. I hadn't even realized it! I felt beholden to him for seeing more than I thought was there.

We talked some more. He was a software entrepreneur. He was on the cutting edge. He was going to release something soon that would be on every computer desktop in the world. It was almost frightening him, this imminent success. He felt he ought to relax and enjoy the slow lane for now.

"There's a show of Woodies today on the wharf," he said. "Want to go down and take a look?"

"Woodies?"

"The original surfermobiles. The Ford wagons with actual oak panels. My childhood dream car."

It was a beautiful day in this fish town, the water deep

blue and restless with whitecaps, the breeze moving just enough to make everything seem alive. Even the fur on mice shines on days like this. The sparrows enjoy the cool grass on their feet. Gray pelicans gulp air into their salty beaks. We sauntered on the wharf for a few hours, our voices lapping at each other like the small bay waves beneath us. We never let up for a second. We ate fresh shrimp with horseradish in little cups and considered every Woody that had made the trip to our wharf. Each stood proud. The beauty of the waxed wood and the effort it had taken to preserve the vehicle in mint condition startled me with the range of human energy. While some people were splitting atoms or untangling DNA, others were shining up their Woodies. Both important in the overall scheme. But what was I doing yet that counted?

As we walked off the wharf, I started to wonder if I could ever quake in circles around this man. It seemed a possibility. Something about him was alluring and unknowable.

"It won't be long before we'll be able to see and hear everything at our desks that we see and hear right here," he said.

"But what about the way the wind feels and the smell of it?" I asked.

"Or the feel of human skin?"

I reached out and touched his arm. It was warm and covered with hair. It had a scar on it, and the muscle stuck out like a blade. "Are *you* real?" I asked.

"I can assure you that I am," he said.

This man brought me a bouquet of dahlias the size of

baby heads the next time I saw him. And though we had a little ceremony, and had Will, and lived together a few years, I had basically married the first person who was nice to me when I was down. It was a mistake, and painful to realize it. Sure, Will and I've not been without our hard times. But we're doing all right. Meanwhile, my sister went to a baroque music festival and met a statistics professor. Is that any better?

●

That night a cool breeze blew in from the sea. We returned all the food and dishes to the kitchenette, and Jiao bought us a pizza to say thanks. The inspection was a success. Will and I could stay on. But something was bothering me, and in my bed I tossed and turned like a netted fish. Finally I gave up trying to sleep, rolled out of bed, and made myself a cup of cocoa. And I must have woken up my sister, because soon she materialized in her flannel pajamas in the hall.

"You all right?" she said.

"Yeah," I said. "How about you?"

"I couldn't sleep either," she said.

"Want some?" I said.

"Might as well," she said.

We padded back into the fake kitchen, and I put another mug of water into the microwave. I watched it going around and around. And then my sister said, "I know this is an intrusive thing to say, but I wish you wouldn't always act like everything's great, even when it's not."

"Me?" I said. "Why would I do that?"

"I don't know," she said. "Why would you?"

I licked the cocoa off my lips and said, "How am I acting like it's great?"

"I don't know," she said. "I guess I feel like I can't talk to you about your existence. You seem defensive about things."

"By the way, why *isn't* it great?" I said.

"God! Forgive me if I say this place seems a little less than ideal."

"Less than ideal, sure, but no worse than where Mom and I lived before you were born."

The microwave pinged. I brought out the mug and added the brown powder from the pouch, stirred and observed the granules dissolve, then presented it with a few clumps still floating on top to my sister. She slurped. "Ouch," she said.

"Careful," I said.

"How come you never told me about you and Jiao?" she said next.

"Me and Jiao?"

"That you guys went out together!"

"That," I said. "Well, it wasn't anything. How'd you dig that up?"

"Today when he was putting back the wall thing and you were out shopping, we all got to talking."

"Oh. That's kind of disturbing. What did he say?"

"Nothing specific, but I could tell."

What was she getting at? "It was just a few dates and a few kisses," I said. "No big deal."

"Well, I got the feeling it was to him."

"No, he's just lonely and letting off steam."

"But he seems so nice! And he has those nice kids, and he's in the same situation you are. And he owns this house!"

"*So?*"

"Why did you leave Boston anyway? You loved working on that magazine."

When I looked at my sister, standing in her pajamas in my pseudo-kitchen, her hair messed up like when she was little, I couldn't help it that I still saw her as a kid. "What's bothering you, anyway?"

"I wish you and Will would come live near us," she said. "Now that I see you here, I just don't understand."

"You think my world here means nothing to me?"

"No, of course not. It just seems—" She couldn't finish.

"What? It seems what?"

"I don't think Mom would be very happy about it," she said.

"What makes you so sure? Wouldn't she be happy that I'm reasonably happy?"

"Yeah, but doesn't it seem she'd be asking you the same questions I have been?" she said.

"So you're just stepping in on her behalf?"

"Something like that," my sister said.

●

After our mother's stroke—which had been sudden, and complete, an aneurism the size of a rock, Roy at her side when she called out *Wait, something's wrong, I don't feel right*—my sister and I took a trip to visit her then-boyfriend at Tulane University in New Orleans. It seemed like a good idea to go on a trip just then.

To save money we signed up for one of those driveaway cars packed full of someone else's television, stereo, sewing machine, and boxes of books, and we drove there from New York in under two days. She didn't like it that I drove so fast, and I didn't like it that she complained, but mostly we were quiet or we cried all the way. About as grim as a 1,129-mile drive in a car full of someone else's stuff could be. Relatively speaking, it was a relief to get to her boyfriend's fraternity house and sack out on the rancid floor of the lounge.

I wasn't happy being there, but I wasn't happy anywhere. I didn't know what I would do with myself next. I thought about Roy, traveling around the world to get his mind on straight. I thought of the sterile, doctorly way my grandmother took the news. There was a coil of anger in me, a sense of *all for nothing* over everything I'd ever accomplished. *For nothing at all.* And not a thing could convince me otherwise. Walking around that city alone, eyes stinging in the flinty air, I found myself one day caught up in a bellicose crowd. Mardi Gras had begun. A parade was thundering past. I ducked into a bar to wait it out. There were men in this bar with the seats of their pants cut out and no underwear on, as well as some others in taffeta party dresses with their blubbery chests pushed up into hairy cleavages. Everybody was drinking up a fit. It had been a few months to the day since Roy called from the emergency room and broke the news, and I ordered a Bloody Mary. A thin man who looked bland compared to the others sat next to me and tried to convince me to let him read my veins. The bartender said, He's the real thing, little girl, and an older woman at the bar came straight over and said, I must watch this. He's a legend around here. He won't do this for just anyone, you know.

I said I didn't have the money for such an honor and the woman said, I'll pay. And she inserted a twenty into the pocket on his chest.

So the thin man chose my left arm, took my hand, rolled up the sleeve of my sweater (it was cold in New Orleans that February), and then began to trace the blue lines up and down my skin. It tickled. I tried to relax. Soon I felt warm all over. He began to tell me about my future. He said my destiny was unlike the destiny of anyone in my family history. He said I was someone with immense inner strength. He said I'd traveled many miles to get where I was now—metaphorically, of course—and that I would crawl on my knees, if I had to, to get to the place I was going. Nothing would get in my way. I laughed. He was totally full of it. He obviously didn't know anything about me. Then suddenly the man grew concerned. The woman dragged intently on her cigarette, one of her ankles turned in, and she nearly toppled over. The man tried to roll my sweater farther up my arm. He pushed my sleeve into my armpit. He was looking at the high white part of my innermost arm. He pressed on my skin as if to see better. He said he was looking at something mysterious.

What is it? I asked impatiently.

I get the feeling, he said, that when you get to this place it's going to confuse you. You're not going to understand why you're there. It will feel all wrong. You'll feel lost. But don't give up. With great leaps of faith, you'll find your way.

Great, I thought. A small crowd had gathered around. The woman who'd paid for this gave me a pat on the shoulder. Beer was a heavy vapor in the air, horns blasted out on the street, and I suddenly experienced a wave of claustrophobia. Thanking the vein reader I pushed my way out, and on a balcony across the street a woman was stripping, flinging her clothes down into the crowd. In moments she was topless. And the clog of people around me roared. I wanted to go back and find my sister. But while I was stuck between one person and the next, shoulder to shoulder, gazing up at the breasts, which were exposed like two pale eggs abandoned in a nest, I suddenly realized it was true I was at an important crossroads, and that my sister's boyfriend was lucky to have such a forward-thinking, energetic person in his life, dealing with things much better than I ever would, and that this woman up on the balcony held the enviable place out of the fray because she was willing *in her own way* to move forward and share something of her real self, and that until I was able to do this, I would always be down here—metaphorically, of course—suffocating.

In one of those mysterious revelations that only last a moment but are utterly elaborate and complete, I thought I finally had a new understanding about my life. It had to do with the last conversation I'd had with my mother the night before she died, which had been a normal, everyday talk, but which had ended with her just happening to say, "I love you to pieces, you wonderful girl." Wasn't it lucky, to have that the last thing she ever said to me? And then there were her ashes, suspended now in the stratosphere, taken by Kathy and Roy and me to the edge of Cape Royal; as they fanned out on the updraft, I'd seen that place as if for the first time.

(So much of the near past had been a blur. The only positive thing I did during that time was take a night class at the Cambridge Adult Center. There I laughed peckishly at just about everything that poetry teacher of mine said, pathetic in my need to cheer up. Just the word *ham*, for example, because one night our class went out to eat, and with a glazed ham steak glistening on my plate, he had urged me to fling it into the center of the restaurant, and to prove my artistic spontaneity I'd done it. Everyone in the class roundly approved. But here I was supposed to be having some kind of life, and flinging a ham steak in a restaurant in Harvard Square was pretty much the most distinguished thing I'd managed to do.)

All the way back to the frat house, I barely registered the bodies I pushed against, the noise, the smells, that's how buoyed I was by this nebulous good feeling and the fortune I'd been told. A shrill wind blew down the tunnels of the gray city streets off Lake Ponchartrain, but I barely felt it. I'm glad I was in such a positive frame of mind when I found Kathy, because she had just broken up with her high-school sweetheart, the very person we had driven all this way to see. My sister is a very careful person. She keeps all her receipts and parts her hair as if cutting a diamond. It's hard to believe such a careful person would have gone so far out of her way just to break up with someone, but that shows how out-of-sorts we both were at the time.

We packed up, decided to leave that very afternoon, and found a driveaway car going north to Richmond, Virginia, from where we'd take a train. On and on we drove, well into the night, both of us drained. At some point I fully opened my eyes and said, "Are you all right?"

"Not really," she replied.

I could see we were no longer on the interstate. It was a two-lane road alive with the sound of crickets and fresh with the smell of grass. "Are we lost?" I said.

"I'm tired and I'm looking for a place to stay," my sister said, with an edge.

It was then that I considered what the vein reader had said to me and realized it might be all right if we were lost. Maybe the more lost the better. Finding our destiny, and so on. It was in that spirit that I looked ahead and saw the tall man wearing bell-bottoms standing near the stop sign. He was laughing and wearing a hat. And for some reason I was filled with a disproportionate feeling of pleasure at the sight of him in the headlights. A man standing by a stop sign! A laughing man. At nearly midnight! Not everyone is tucked in at this hour after all; I liked that. Not everyone retires to a comfortable bed. Would he stick out his thumb, ask us for a ride? What would my sister think? Would she step on the gas or stop and let him in? Who would he be, what was his story? Was he a civilized person or just a bum? I'd get her to stop; we'd get this man to talk. Who knows what stories he could tell. But as the car slowed down, I realized the man in the bell-bottoms was not a man but a defunct tree, all gnarled trunk, a few wild suckers sprouting from the base. Hard to believe, but tears stung my eyes.

"Maybe you'd better drive," my sister said then. "I guess I really am too tired. I thought that was a man standing there."

"Wearing bell-bottoms?"

"Now that you mention it, yes, it looked like he was wearing embroidered pants."

"That's funny, I thought it was a man too."

"You did?" my sister said, pulling over. "Didn't he look nice?" We both laughed.

I was thinking how amazing it was that we'd both been open to the possibility that a laughing man in bell-bottoms standing by a stop sign in the middle of the night might help us move on with our lives, and just then she held my hand.

I was sad when my sister and the statistics professor went back to New York. I'd miss her no matter what she thought of my life, and I always did, because I knew that, owing to a long series of bumps and twists in the past, we'd never live in the same house, town, or state again. That's just how it would be. And after they were gone, it wasn't long before I saw that I was walking through my life without my usual good cheer, even at the things I normally enjoyed most, like talking over Will's day with him when I met him at the bus stop, like going back to my bedroom in the morning for my moment alone. Instead, I felt like a fog had come in the windows from the sea and entered my thoughts, and nothing made sense anymore.

Still, after I'd walked a few hours more that day, it dawned on me that in many ways I was happier than I ever had been. Really. Or maybe as happy as I'd always been, deep down. I saw the water twinkling and the sun glinting and the birds resting on sandbars and realized I was enjoying it so much it was almost shocking. I had passed all the beach houses long ago and was well along on a stretch I had never set foot on before. It was flat and empty for miles ahead, with only a few gulls dipping here and there to keep me company. The waves were knee high at best, the widest part of the bay, making about as much sound as a bowl of soup. There was a breeze, smelling of salt and seaweed, like a child's breath on a summer afternoon.

At the bus stop that morning, Will had said, "I want to have a zoo arranged alphabetically, and especially a lot of animals that start with U."

"What starts with U?" I said.

"Uakaris, ungulates, stuff like that. If you wanted to be reincarnated with green bones, you know what you'd have to be?"

"No, what?"

"A xenopus."

"Neat," I said.

"You know what's a nonillion?" he said.

"What?"

"There's only one thing that's a nonillion," he said. "It's how many live things there are on earth."

It was time to turn around and go home.

If our tribe had been driven off the earth, if Will and I were the only ones left, then we'd eventually have to learn the customs of those around us. Of course. We were cooperative, reasonable types. But would there be any reason to rush?

acknowledgments

For various forms of support and encouragement, I would like to thank: C. Michael Curtis, John Chandler, Carole Conn, James R. Cox, Margaret M. Cox, Dave Eggers, Peter Farkas, Amanda Field, Margaret Forbes, Reginald Gibbons, Syed Haider, Deborah Hansen, Bill Henderson, Richard Huffman, Howard Junker, Kathryn Kefauver, Richard Lange, Jeffrey Lependorf, Wendy Lesser, Roger McKenzie, Katherine Minton, Andrew X. Pham, Carl Recknagel, Mildred Recknagel, Jay Schaefer, Isaiah Sheffer, George H. Smith, Elizabeth Spence, Randy Splitter, Sandy Tanaka, Alfredo Véa, Shalom Victor, Vito Victor, Dan White, Kirby Wilkins, the Woodhams family, and Christopher Wrench.

To my wonderful agent, Kim Witherspoon, as well as Eleanor Jackson and Alexis Hurley at InkWell Management, go my thanks for their generosity and belief.

To my brilliant editor, Lee Boudreaux, and to Daniel

Acknowledgments

Menaker, Laura Ford, Kate Blum, and Vincent La Scala at Random House, go my thanks for their guidance and vision.

To my friend Donka Farkas, who has been there every step of the way, my great thanks.

To my lifelong friends Roberta Gignac Montgomery and Patricia Stacey, to my sister Emily Cox, and to my boys Nick and Stuart, my deep gratitude for inspiring me in so many ways.

Above all, to Steve Woodhams, for his insightful readings of this book and much more, my love and thanks.

STOP THAT GIRL

Elizabeth McKenzie

A Reader's Guide

A Conversation with Elizabeth McKenzie

Q: How much of *Stop That Girl* is autobiographical?

Elizabeth McKenzie: I think of *Stop That Girl* as an alternate universe, but parts did end up being pretty auto-biographical. For some reason the image of Frankenstein's monster comes to mind—a real arm here, a real leg there, but when sewn together, something "other" emerges. This material seemed to demand a certain amount of attention to a past I knew. The matter came up of missing certain people and wanting to hear from them again. I'll have to admit to a bit of grave robbing here.

Q: I understand you actually met Allen Ginsberg, and that the real-life encounter was much like the one in the book. Can you tell us more?

EM: One night, my best friend Roberta and I borrowed a hulking wreck of a car in order to drive Ginsberg around town and to Baba Ram Dass' (or was it Bagavan Das'?) house one night. I looked up to him as if he were the Abra-ham Lincoln of his time. From the garbage-filled backseat this great voice graciously replied to all the naïve questions we peppered him with.

Q: And did you really find Bob Dylan's hose nozzle?

EM: One night, my best friend Roberta and I did end up being shown around Bob Dylan's new house by a couple of carpenters finishing up the job. The nozzle ended up in my pocket. After a while, I started to feel kind of dumb about it. I doubted he had gone out and bought it himself. But I still liked it a lot, compared to other nozzles.

Q: Ann has some very complicated relationships with the adults in her life, starting with her mother. Would you agree that the roles are reversed in this relationship?

EM: Not exactly reversed, but certainly gnarled.

Q: Dr. Frost, Ann's grandmother, is a spectacular character. Definitely a bit troubled yet, at the same time, very attentive to Ann—albeit in her own, misguided way. Can you explain this?

EM: I've noticed that a lonely adult can often let down her guard with a child in a way that she can't with her peers, and this is the case with the relationship between Dr. Frost and Ann. When I was a child, I often found myself hanging around with lonely adults who seemed to like talking to me. Naturally, this made me feel special and good, but whether or not they were models of mental health, I don't know.

Q: Is Dr. Frost based on someone from your life?

EM: I have just begun to plumb the depths of the very strange person who was my grandmother—my Dr. Frost. A grandmother for me is not a warm and cozy gray-haired being but a prickly snarling ball of mania and misguided schemes. The kind of person whose acquaintances take you aside and whisper, "Call me if you ever need to talk."

Q: One of the most dramatic scenes is the confrontation between Ann's mother and Dr. Frost after Dr. Frost "kidnaps" Ann. What was the motivation behind writing this?

EM: I was very interested in the aftermath of such an episode, no doubt in part because it mirrors an actual situation in my own family—after which my mother and grandmother were out of touch for thirty years. It's amazing how years of fury can stay under control until one day something happens, such as this, and the whole relationship blows up, and there's no turning back.

Q: What do you think caused the change in Ann's feelings toward her stepfather, Roy Weeks? Is he more of a parent than Ann's own mother?

EM: Roy wins Ann over through simple acts of kindness and honesty. It's no surprise that someone in his position can be more of a parent than an actual one. There are a lot of great non-parents out there, people who make a huge difference to people who need them.

Q: Your work also carries with it a very strong sense of dislocation. Is this theme borrowed from your own experience?

EM: Yes. A big theme in my own childhood was that we were always in the wrong place, and that we had to keep looking for the "right" place. It was hard to define what would be the right place. It had nothing to do with schools or job opportunities. "The neighbors" always seemed to have something to do with the problem. A mystery like this, something you don't really understand about your life, will keep you going as you write.

Q: Do you think a certain California ethos infuses your work?

EM: I'm not conscious of the California angle and wouldn't cultivate it. If I tried to, I think it would wreck everything.

It wasn't until I went to school for a year in a foreign country (which happened to be Australia) that I realized there was anything special about Los Angeles in the world's view. There, I seemed to be an object of undue fascination, and kids were asking me questions about Hollywood and Disneyland and the Manson family. I admitted I didn't know anyone in the Manson family, but that I had definitely been to Disneyland, and that Hollywood was not a single building but a whole town. I had a furry coat with big toggles on it that I'd been embarrassed of at home, but which everyone there seemed to think was extremely hip. Looking back, I realize that *they* were the hip ones. The kids I met there were much less cut from the mold.

Questions and Topics for Discussion

1. How does the setting of California shape *Stop That Girl*? How might the novel be different if it were set in another region?

2. Discuss the social backdrop to these stories. How does the culture of the sixties and seventies help shape Ann's identity?

3. In the first chapter, Ann takes off running with her baby sister. What provokes her to do this? Do you understand her motives in this instant?

4. Explore Dr. Frost's effect on Ann and her family. How does Ann's mother's relationship with Dr. Frost compare to Ann's relationship with her grandmother? What do you think Dr. Frost's motives are in regards to her relationship to Ann? Is she merely eccentric, or do you think she has deeper psychological problems? Does Ann or her mother resemble Dr. Frost in any way?

5. *Stop That Girl* has the unusual format of consistently skipping time between chapters. How did this structure

function as a way to explore the turning points in Ann's life, and how did it affect your reading experience?

6. In "Life on Comet," how does Ann view her mother's depression? How does Ann's perception of her mother change in "We Know Where We Are, But Not Why" when her family is in Arizona?

7. Many reviewers have called Ann Ransom a surprising and original character. How does she differ from other female characters you've encountered in contemporary fiction?

8. At the end of "Look Out, Kids," Ann says, "It all could have been so much different." What does Ann wish were different? In the broadest sense, why wasn't it?

9. What messages about family does *Stop That Girl* send? How does McKenzie define the variables of family?

10. How does McKenzie use humor to express Ann's worldview?

11. In "S.O.S.," Ann describes her attraction to her boy-friend, Bart, as originating when she realized "He didn't like anybody, felt superior, and coming from where I did I was used to this kind of person. One thing led to another" (154). What does she mean with this statement?

12. Roy is one of the few loyal men in *Stop That Girl*. Why is he so dedicated to Ann's mother and his family? How

would you characterize the other male characters that appear throughout the narrative?

13. Ann finds herself in an uncomfortable situation with her employer in "The Possible World." Beyond the immediate circumstances, what do you think brought her to this low point?

14. How and where does the theme of being "last of the tribe" surface in this narrative?

15. Throughout the novel, Ann and her family constantly move. Why can't Ann's mother settle in one place? What effect does this upheaval have on the rest of the family?

16. How would you compare Ann's personality at the end of the novel to her character at age seven? Which elements of her personality have changed, and which have essentially remained the same?

17. What are your predictions for Ann's future? How do you think she'll live her life?

ELIZABETH McKENZIE was raised in Los Angeles. Her writing has appeared in *The New York Times, Best American Nonrequired Reading, Pushcart Prize XXV, Other Voices, Threepenny Review, TriQuarterly,* and *ZYZZYVA;* and her work has been recorded for National Public Radio's "Selected Shorts." A former staff editor at *The Atlantic Monthly,* she lives in Santa Cruz, California.

Visit the author's website: www.stopthatgirl .com

About the Type

This book was set in Fairfield, the first typeface from the hand of the distinguished
American artist and engraver Rudolph Ruzicka (1883–1978). In its structure Fairfield
displays the sober and sane qualities of the
master craftsman whose talent has long been
dedicated to clarity. It is this trait that accounts for the trim grace and vigor, the spir-
ited design and sensitive balance, of this
original typeface.

Rudolph Ruzicka was born in Bohemia
and came to America in 1894. He set up his
own shop, devoted to wood engraving and
printing, in New York in 1913 after a varied
career working as a wood engraver, in photo-
engraving and banknote printing plants, and
as an art director and freelance artist. He de-
signed and illustrated many books, and was
the creator of a considerable list of individual
prints—wood engravings, line engravings on
copper, and aquatints.